# Epicharis.

# Epicharis.

## /grievechronic\

### Angel Brynner

KokoPelliMa Press

Library of Congress
Cataloging-in-Publication Data
Brynner, Angel
Epicharis, grievechronic/ Angel Brynner
Library of Congress control number:2019956719
ISBN: 978-1-950077-04-5
EBOOK ISBN  978-1-950077-05-2



Cover artwork and book design by AOLAB
Additional image credit:macrovector_official & Luis Molinero
Website : http://www.GRIEVECHRONIC.com

KOKOPELLIMA PRESS

# Epicharis


…Even if it takes all night ,
If you go down
get back up
and fucking fight.

*For Love,*

*and those who know better.*

**chapter one**

As soon as Anukai hit the outside air  she knew she wasn't going to make it to the library. Adam sheepishly waved at her from the other side of the fenced in lot.

As they cut through side streets in silence the fact that Adam had given up permeated the atmosphere.

They dodged into the woods that crawled  alongside the reservoir and picked their way up the ravine that became a nature preserve at the bottom of the Shaker Lakes. After an eternity of bored nods of recognition  towards each other due to the toxic friendship between their mothers they'd stumbled across one  another in these woods what felt like lifetimes ago, both hiding from the madness that tried to devour them at home.

He was her best friend and her first kiss. Anukai blush grinned and shoved Adam as they traipsed to the patch of grass she had experienced her first stabs of puppy love in, sprawled on his stomach as they both looked up at thick, lumbering, acid-white clouds and dreamt of running away.

They laid their coats on the ground and crumbled against each other as he pulled out toffifays, lemonheads, sweet-tarts and whachamacalits for them to feast on. The woods were always more quiet than made sense smack dab in the middle of the city. He pulled out Dr. Peppers and Mountain Dews to go with the cheese-steak hoagies he'd picked up at the Galleria downtown for them.

Anukai started to cry as she looked down at their last supper. She knew it was only a matter of time. He couldn't handle it at home anymore. Knowing that didn't break her heart any less.

"It's going to be Me… not my evil mother or my deranged father," Adam whispered, "I won't give either of them the satisfaction of me killing them for what they've done or the pleasure of not dying by each other's hands."

Adam knew Anukai would not tell. Especially after what happened when their friend Michael, another kid of their parental pack of Toastmistresses, took his own life.

Adam reached over and clumsily wiped Anukai's tears. "I won't say don't cry~but be happy for me. I'm finally out," he whispered. He raised his can of pop as the sun came out from behind the clouds and illuminated the clearing the same way it did the first time they broke bread together in it, knowing they were safe with each other, forever. He shoved her gently, put her Dr. Pepper in her hand and cleared his throat.

"So… to US~!" he sang out happily. "And To breaking out of hell!"

"One way or another," Anukai whispered and tried to laugh through her tears before she threw her pop aside and grabbed her best friend.

"You're the best thing that happened to me in hell on earth!" she whispered harshly against the side of his face.

" I know," Adam sniffed and laughed through his own tears. "So they failed after all. We found each other anyway, right?"

" Both of us  lasted longer than they ever said we respectively would," Anukai whispered defiantly.

They hugged each other and looked up at the sun honoring their last meal together.

"See you on the other side," Adam whispered as they parted ways.
"One way or another," Anukai said like she always did.

At the last minute Adam leaned in and gently kissed his first and last love goodbye. Anukai laughed as she cried then wrinkled up her nose just like she'd done the first time their lips had brushed.

"You still taste like Red Hots and Sweet-tarts,"
"I just ate three boxes and two rolls of them, remember?" Adam crowed back, same as he did the first time. "I love you Anukai," Adam whispered as he hugged his best friend one more time as the sun went down.

" I know," Anukai sniffed as they both laughed.
"Not a decimation, right?"he growled against the side of her head of wild hair.

"Nope, it's a celebration~" she whispered.

**chapter two**

Danise closed the door to the room she grew up in and leaned against it.

She looked around listlessly, then stared blankly out the window. There was no part of her day that wasn't exhausting, from the job she was too grateful to have to hate to the well-meaning yet intrusive press of the prayer warriors that kept a hedge of protection around her and Gabryl in the spirit since both of her parents had passed on. Whether he appreciated it or not.

The sigh that rattled her chest as she sat down on the bed to take off her shoes was all the beasts pressed against the far side of the glass needed to start up once again.

It started as a whisper and grew, peppering the periphery of her thoughts.

"Bannister sees the sanctified sham you are and you know it-" It hissed against the window.

Weary-eyed, Danise looked up upon impact of the barb. A faint ring of condensation bloomed and faded on the outside of the window as she gently pressed her left thumb up into the bony indent below her brow.

"None of them like you-" whispered another as its shadow seeped out of the corner her bed was pushed into. "They all know what you were no matter what you say you are now…" it hissed.

She felt herself crumbling under the onslaught, the words required to fight them just not coming.

She grabbed a pillow, folded over and cried into her lap. Emboldened, her tormentors slid through the atmosphere into full view and surrounded her as her shoulders shook from the force of her silent sobs.

They brought up every old pain and fear they'd ever known Danise to have had and whipped her with  all of it, allowing her no peace.  She curled up on the bed, crippled with guilt, wracked by memories running roughshod over her.

"And now, you're gonna lose him too-" the one who'd seeped into the space through the floorboards sneered.

"If you think  he's out there getting up to anything  better than what you used to, you're even more of a fool than we already knew-"

"He's…a good kid-" Danise whispered  hoarsely against the spiritual attack.

"A good kid you dragged through Hell in your wake-" another laughed. "He's already ours, it's just a matter of time, thanks to you-"

Danise sat up bolt-straight as if the accusation had kicked her in the teeth. But it connecting  turned the tide inside of her.

"He…is a GOOD. Kid." Gabryl's mother growled defiantly. The demons stepped back as she hopped off the bed  and began to pace through them, muttering declarations between heartfelt prayers of protection over her now teenaged son.

"The damage is already done, Danise~"a tormentor hissed as she kept claiming Gabryl as covered by the blood.

 She wouldn't stop. Every time  she said it the words landed like right hooks, knocking the spirits back towards the walls, windows and floors they'd arrogantly come through trying to drag her down like before, head-first.

"Your declarations mean Nothing!" roared the one who'd led the charge against her.

"In the name of Jesus," Danise howled softly.

The demons looked at each other in alarm then pressed back towards her menacingly, doubting she believed enough for the power embedded in that name to matter.

She stood her ground as they lobbed insults at her.
"In the NAME of Jesus, I Declare my SON is Protected from ALL the ways of the devil, That my words will not return to me void! I Plead The BLOOD over him, over this space!"

It was as if a spiritual bomb went off.  Blood splattered everywhere, flicking across the twisted with shock countenances of the accusers, burning them like acid.

They screamed  and fled through shadows and glass, not one able to cross the threshold to gain deeper entry to the home. Danise fell to her knees, prayers slipping out the corner of her mouth as she crawled back to her bed for the nap she'd needed hours before she'd finally been able to get home in the first place, rest that would be the only thing to help her make it through the rest of the night if it came, outside of Jesus.

She rose an hour later. Refreshed, Danise pulled on her coat to go grab groceries before Gabryl got home. The walls  shared by neighboring apartments weakly tried to remind her he hadn't been back in three days to no avail.

"The past is over-" she whispered to no one other than herself. "Treat it like it's over. He's a good kid. In the name of Jesus, he'll be home when I get back."

**chapter three**

The diatribe in the background continued. Anukai washed another pile of dishes left in the sink from food the mother had made for herself without any acknowledgement of the hunger of her teenaged kids.  As she blankly dunked her hands into the soapy water on autopilot she felt a heart-beat entwined with her own begin to fade.

Across the way in the TV room the mother gossiped about how Adam, the "lost"  son of one of her friends had tried to kill himself earlier that day. He was in the hospital running up bills as his parents tried to make  their grief look believable in front of the concerned doctors.

"He's supposedly lost so much blood that there is almost no hope or point..." the mother crowed. Anukai's mother laughed about all her friend had done to deserve the grief that the loss of a child would normally cause. "But the  biggest drama is over his daddy," the mother purred into the phone.

"He vehemently refused to give blood in order to save his own son's life at first! Fear of needles, he said! Got shamed into it by the doctor only to find out the boy ain't even his- Giiiirlll~"

"He stormed out of the hospital, all "I want a divorce! And you're getting nothing! In front of everybody! Yes! She called me crying about it-" the mother cackled, waving it off, "then she wouldn't even get off the phone to go Be with her dying son- I couldn't Wait to tell you!"

Anukai stacked the dishes in a daze, moving onto the obscene pile of glasses the mother had accrued in less than three hours home as the beat she felt against her inner ear got fainter.  She gritted her teeth as the mother complained about planning the wake/potluck under the hawk-like eyes of their so-called friends showing out for front-row seats to the spectacle of the latest woman in their ranks losing a child to suicide and gaining access to prematurely paid-out life insurance, right as the husband she'd repeatedly cheated on was finally divorcing her.

The mother laughed out loud. "I should be so lucky for her to crawl off somewhere and die-"

Anukai absently grasped the rim of a glass underwater as everything around her paused. The heartbeat and faint-breathing stopped at the same time as a bright light  exploded in front of her eyes. She saw herself grab the dirty butcher knife on the counter and stab her vindictive mother in the chest repeatedly, a tell-tale demonic sixth finger rupturing the side of her stabbing hand as she butchered her on the couch.

In a flash, what felt like the grip of a hand shot through the water and wrapped itself around Anukai's wrist to stop her.

*"She's not Worth it- and you are not like them-"* Adam's voice boomed in her head, using the last of his spirit to stop her. Everything in front of Anukai went red as the glass she held onto broke and jabbed through the side of her hand right where the demonic digit would have been.

Anukai looked down at the bloody, sudsy water, lifted her hand and stoically pulled the hunk of glass still rammed in it down and out, letting the spiritual bloodline marker fall back into the sink and disintegrate  in her mind's eye, then dropped the chunk of glass into the sink.

In shock, Anukai wrapped a wet kitchen towel around her hand and slowly walked into the TV room towards the mother.

"Yeah, I'm sure her nosy ass is probably eavesdropping now. Yeah, he was her friend… No- fuck her- hopefully she'll be joining him soon enough-" the mother bellowed for show and then cracked up.

"What!" the mother barked without even looking up, feeling Anukai's presence. "What do you want?"

"Take me… to the hospital." Anukai whispered.
"Why?!" the mother snapped.  "So you can see your little-"

Anukai didn't even flinch. "Take… me to the hospital."she said again.

The mother started to show out with her bemused friend still on the line. "Who do you think you are?!" she began, oblivious to the blood that now dripped onto the floor as she ranted.

Anukai numbly watched the mother snarling and realized that she was about to pass out. She turned on her heels and headed for the back door without saying a word right before everything went black.

"Don't you walk away from me when I am talking to you-"

The last thing Anukai heard was the mother screaming at the top of her lungs, full of  real concern for the first time in Anukai's entire life as she crumpled to the floor.

**chapter four**

Gabryl sat at the desk in what had been his grandmother's room what felt like a lifetime ago trying to do his homework.

He had been gone for three days while his now completely sanctified mother had been caught up in yet another revival, and he was sure there was going to be hell to pay soon as she saw he was back.

The numbers scrawled across the page only made sense to him when he  translated them to music in his mind's eye. Him finding the song in everything was what kept him breathing as he pushed through the carnage that the city blocks he'd grown up on had only recently tried to recover from, no matter the pushback from the beasts that had fattened themselves up on the community they'd cannibalized during the drug wars.

Danise came in with a song  in her heart from the one true lord. Her atonal rendition of it set Gabryl's teeth on edge. She'd won the war against drugs with Jesus but lost her voice in the process, and didn't care.

She saw the sliver of light from her son's room as she walked to hers and paused, unconsciously girding herself for the battle that had become so routine between them that though afraid for his safety,  the days she came home from the prayer group both her parents had belonged to and found the apartment empty, she was a little relieved.

She opened her mouth to address his three day absence on auto-pilot but the Lord shushed her.

Danise looked up at the ceiling, nodded obediently as his childhood nickname rose awkwardly in her, a name she'd spent a good seven years too broken to call out to him with.

Shaken by the sweetness of it on her lips, she whispered her prayer right outside his door.

"Thank you for returning my Gabloomy home safe, I know you will never stop watching over him, in the name of Jesus, thank you." she repeated again and again.

## chapter five

"What the fuck did you do?" the mother yelled, finally seeing the blood-soaked towel. She hovered over Anukai and hysterically grabbed at it until the hand of the unconscious girl fell to the ground with a slick thud.

She pressed her face to Anukai's to see if she was breathing. "Wake up! Wake up! " the mother wailed as she roughly pulled at Anukai until she got her up onto her feet and slumped her over the counter next to the back patio.

The mother raced over to the kitchen and gagged at the pile of bloodied glass and soapy water that filled the sink. She looked away as she turned on the cold faucet, quickly wet another towel, ran over to Anukai and squeezed the water from it onto her face.

"Wake up!" she screamed and slapped Anukai. The girl came to a bit as the mother stared into her obviously in shock face.

"Come on!" the mother yelled and dragged a groggy Anukai out the sliding doors, down the patio steps and leaned her on the hood of the car, then ran back into the house frantically searching for her car keys.

"God-Don't let her die-please! God-Please!" she yelled. Sixteen years after the birth of Anukai the Mother morphed into *Her* mother for the first time as she dropped to her knees in the pool of her daughter's blood. "Just let me get her to the hospital-Please,God-"

She suddenly heard the keys loudly scrape across the counter and drop to the kitchen floor.

Her mother grabbed them, ran out and put Anukai in the car.

"Just stay awake, Anukai- don't go to sleep-" her mother chattered  as she ran around, jumped in and sped to St. Luke's Hospital, babbling the entire time to keep Anukai conscious, feeling her black out again on the way. She knew she couldn't stop and that  she didn't know how much blood she'd lost.

Anukai's mother slammed on the horn as she careened into the parking lot.

**chapter six**

Gabryl felt his mother through the door but refused to look up, bracing for another round.  But she didn't knock. Old battles die hard but eventually they end.

Gabryl sat there and listened to her whispering and got  angrier as it dawned on him. "...she's freaking praying? For ME-?" Gabryl snarled, insulted. "She's praying for *me-*"

The rage he'd quietly carried over his mother ramming her "Get out of hell free with Jesus" card in his  face in the aftermath of his grandmother having passed away crackled across the surface of his soul.

"Jesus just let her forget all of it- Well- well you know what?"he sputtered angrily, "That shit she is freed from I had to live through as a kid because of her! She- she gets to be fine but I still see those piles of drugged people in my fucking dreams-" he yelled, standing up faster than he should have.

Gabryl looked up in alarm as the room started to spin like it had when he'd come to in the alley as a kid, screaming as blood poured out of his chest.

"...What- the H-hell?!" he slurred as he crumpled to the floor.

He landed so hard on his nose that blood spread across the floorboards underneath his face.

**chapter seven**

Paramedics rushed out. Anukai's mother raced around to open the door and her daughter crumbled out into her arms, her jeans thick with the blood that had continued to flow. The cut on the side of her hand gaped down to almost the center of her wrist.

She began to wail as the paramedics swarmed her and her child, lifting both of them up and away from each other as they slammed Anukai down onto a gurney, strapped an oxygen mask onto her face and rolled her through the doors.

"She- she was washing -my…my dishes- and, it looked like one shattered-" her mother stammered as she stumbled after them.

Nurses grabbed Anukai's mother and tried to calm her down as all the things she'd said and done her child's entire life roared inside her head. An emergency room doctor came out  up and she flung herself at his feet.

"She's going to be fine." he reported gently as he helped her up. "She lost a lot of blood and is going to have a lot of stitches down the side of her left hand once she comes to, but she's didn't cut a nerve and is going to be okay."

Anukai's mother cried on his shoulder until she caught her breath. Suddenly, she wondered if had she even parked the car. "Thank god- thank you doctor-Excuse me, I need to get some air-" she whispered as she wiped away tears and walked to the lot.

The car was left wide open across two handicapped spaces.

She shook her head in disbelief and parked as near as possible to the hospital entrance. It was a quiet night, but the lot was full. Anukai's mother looked up self-consciously, feeling as if she were being watched as she headed back towards the hospital. She looked around.

About ten paces away, a young guy stopped. He pushed his black hoodie off. His shaved head gleamed in the night like a skull as he glared balefully at her. She took a small step away. He mimicked her then smiled roughly.

"That was some performance you put on in there…But we both know you've been waiting for this night all her life, right?" His eyes blacked out as an angry scowl spread across his features. "You just said it before she did it-"*I wish she'd just crawl off somewhere and-*" He cackled. The air around the mother got very thin as the color drained from her face.

"Who- who are you?" she hissed softly.

"Who am I? Come on now! You all but dedicated her to us as soon as you let him plant her in you, let alone got out of you! And tonight, I'm going to pick up what was no more than a inconvenient parasite you ferried into hell on earth as it was-" he hissed back at Anukai's mother. The sensation of pins and needles swarmed her, making her falter. The demon feigned pity.

"Oh…don't tell me you've had a change of heart?" he purred malevolently. The mother stood rooted to the asphalt. "Come on now! You and me? We're… We're fucking family, remember?! Technically, through your blood she's kind of one of ours as it is! Just barely over the line in opposition to it - just needs to be…*groomed* for the service you conscripted her into-damned near dedicated her to-that wolf  Tsunga you picked to feed her to trimmed a lot…but not enough, apparently-"

Anukai's mother swooned a bit at the outright mention of Anukai's childhood molester and looked around nervously for help.

"Oh! *Now* you're too weak to deal with what you did to her for *stealing your husband's love as a fucking baby?!*  After she survived it? Just because she's bleeding out in there?" He waved away her melodrama.  "You wanna feign weakness now? Please! I was there… when you conspired with them, gave them fucking permission… so sell that shit elsewhere! You've had such a direct line to our side all along for a fucking reason, much so we never had to sign shit... But~Don't worry! She'll be fiiine-I'll treat her as good as you did! Let's shake on it-"  The demon extended  an obscenely long hand with six fingers on it to officially seal the deal. Terrified, her mother ran back into the emergency waiting room as the demon laughed behind her.

She made the doctor confirm  that Anukai would be okay and that the cut was nowhere near a suicidal slash, then did her best to wait until they'd let her see her daughter without having a nervous breakdown.

She was so jumpy that the doctor wrote her a prescription for a strong sedative to calm her nerves until Anukai came through.

"She loves her so much-" the nurses murmured to one another, watching her zone out as the pills took hold of her.

"I know- can you imagine how she must feel?"
"Such a lucky child-"
"A mother that cares like that is so rare these days."

## chapter eight

Anukai laid in the sterile hospital room on the seventh floor and waited for the painkiller she'd been shot up with to fade.

The cuss-out over coming home late due to the Last Supper with Adam stung in a way it shouldn't have as she replayed it against what the mother had just done to get her there.

Try as she might, the realities of the two women existing inside of one wouldn't mesh.  The whores, cunts and sluts that the mother had hurtled at the virgin Anukai had been enough to push her over the edge on a good night, but that night had been as far from good as it could possibly have been.

All of her mother's toxic friends doused their kids with the same vitriol over the theft of their shallow, materialistic lives.

Adam was the 13th kid who'd tried to kill himself  after being raised by a pack of  women who back-stabbed one another over the phone as vigilantly as they did at ostentatious pot-lucks that balanced their reserved Toast-Mistress meetings. And it wasn't like tonight's barrage was new. They all had cackled over the fiscally fortunate misfortune of the twelve deaths that had proceeded this one.

But in the pit of snakes called *friends of family*, Adam had been a last light to all of the kids. And his mother had been one of the worst. As Anukai stared at the ceiling she remembered what the mother had said about the blood.

Anukai knew the only dad Adam had ever known had beaten him to a pulp to show dominance when he was little, eventually getting sexual like a violent child militia leader.

She wearily wondered if the depravity of what he'd done to Adam had only registered when he found out they weren't related.

Anukai closed her eyes to all of it, grief blocking her lungs as she passed back out.

## chapter nine

In a room full of machines on the thirteenth floor alone,  Adam came back to life in Anukai's arms. The machines began to slowly beep again.

Both of them were covered in blood,  Adam in the blood she'd found his spirit in and hers, in spite of all that he had viciously drained out of himself.

He inspected what she had done to her hand to be there when he had to let go so he wouldn't die alone as she kissed his face for what he had stopped her from doing. If he hadn't it would have tied her to the demon housed in that mother another round of forevers.

The man in the black hoodie stood at the threshold of the room behind them.  He sniffed the air in search of Adam's signal, a pit stop on the way to Anukai's. "It's time." he whispered gruffly.

 "Wait-" he hesitated, black eyes fading to white in confusion at the scent of both parcels he'd come for separately entwined on the bed in front of his blind eyes.

The machines in the room beeped  faster as a flood of monarch butterflies burst through the window. They swarmed the two blood-soaked teenagers on the bed and blocked their signals from view.

"What?! No!" The man screamed, trapped at the threshold.

A monarch landed on Adam's forehead as he gasped. "Jesus!" he screamed, bewildered.

"Come-" a voice echoed.
"No!" Death screamed.

The room shook as the butterflies shot up from the bed in a cloud, escorting Adam from St. Luke's Hospital across the threshold none can see before their time.

Anukai's blood flaked off of her as she defiantly crawled out the bed and walked through death as if it did not even exist.

She padded barefoot down the hall, bloody footprints evaporating by the time she climbed in the elevator. Death slammed into the elevator's closing doors as she wagged a finger a him.

She found the rest of herself still asleep in the room on the seventh floor, her mother completely sedated, curled up in an uncomfortable chair pulled beside the still breathing body of her eldest daughter as Anukai's Ka eased back in.

**chapter ten**

Danise paced back and forth in her room, egged on to confront him from one side of herself, admonished to trust God and let him be by the other.

She felt the pressure mounting in the room again and charged out of it. "Make dinner. Put some food in you, Danise."

She headed to the kitchen, prepared her seventh day adventist style bland dinner and sat down to eat in silence. Soon she'd have to pray. Go to bed. Pray some more. Get up. Ask for forgiveness and then push back out into the world to do it all again.

It was the ritual that was somewhat saving her, the rigorous commitment to putting it all on the altar in meekness took almost everything out of her as she tried to keep her past sins as far away from her as east was from west.

Not even Gabloomy could stand against the necessity of that.

She paused inside at his nickname rolling across her heart again for the second time in years that day.

He barreled into the kitchen as if he hadn't been MIA for three days, hungry. A crust of blood rimmed his nostril.

"There's food on the stove if you want it. I- Left it for you," Danise said fake-cheerfully. "In case you were back-" she added, a part of her unable to resist.

Gabryl sighed. "Does it have any salt?"

"No…I can't have that anymore but," Danise started, ignoring her son's eye roll as she got up and went to the cabinet, "But I got this for you, just in case-"

She extended a bottle of salt like the peace offering it was after throwing all the seasoning out  of the house without any thought to his taste-buds when she'd done it.

Gabryl looked blankly at the salt in her hand and snarled like she'd rubbed it into the wound she'd acted like she hadn't even comprehended throwing everything away had been to him.

"No thanks, Danise." he grunted and  went towards the cabinet to look for his stash of peanut butter.

"I- I made you food, Gabryl. You don't have to-" Danise started to fuss.

 "No-" Gabryl growled, "You made YOU food. You. You didn't think about me at all. You just thought about God being proud of your sanctified, salt-free show of-"

"I am not going to do this with you, boy- Eat what I made…or don't eat."

Gabryl laughed. "Wow Danise- you- you really think you -of all people- can tell me what to eat?" He spun the top off the peanut butter. " No, see- This," he whispered, "This is peanut butter I bought…for myself…during one of those times there was no food in the house at all, Danise. Remember those times, Danise? Huh? Because I do-"

"Mom." Danise growled, riled. Gabryl looked at his mother like she'd lost it.

"You want me to call YOU Mom?! Nah! You? You're not my mom! I don't know what you did with her…but you are Not my fn mom-" Gabryl hissed evenly.

"Who do you think you're talking to, Gabryl?!" Danise yelled.

"The body snatcher who replaced my mom after she broke Again, leaving me with nobody but-" Gabryl yelled back.
" Do you know that Danise? Huh? Remember her?! She …she went through some shit, yeah, but-"

"I did this for you-" Danise argued.
"You never have done anything for anyone but you!" Gabryl roared. "Aren't you even going to Ask me where I've been?! Huh, mom? Of course you're not! You don't care, just gave me up to Jesus, right? A little indifferent prayer up to the most high and your job as a mother is done, right? My mother would've never not given a-" Gabryl cried out and then stopped himself.

"She…she no longer exists-" Danise whispered, hurt, unable to explain.

"Then neither do I!" Gabryl screamed. "How do you not get it?! That shit still happened! I went through ALL of it WITH you! And you just - oh you're free of it, and everything's for Jesus and your healing- what about me, Danise?! What about the little kid you used to drag in drug dens with you, who had to find you in that shit?! You got a clean slate! Where's mine?! Huh? Ever ask your fucking God that?!"

He looked around angrily. "You know what? Fuck this! I'm done-!"

"Gabloomy, don't-" Danise croaked, on the verge of tears.

"No! Don't you call me that," he seethed. "Not now- not after you stopped calling me that even before she died! Don't you ever call me that again-not after all you've done. Everyone who has a right to call me that name is dead-"

"Gabryl! I understand you're upset but-" Danise did her best to stay calm.

"What are you going to do, Danise? Break again?! This time it's going to be my fault, huh?! Is that it?!"he roared.

"Get out of my-"
"Your parent's house?! That she put my name on too?! Knowing you and your…shit?!" Gabryl looked around, "You know what? Fine! I'm out!"

Gabryl slammed out into the streets.

Danise stood in shock in the kitchen for what seemed like forever, fists clenched.

Something inside her nudged her back to her now cold dinner. She woodenly sat down and obediently chewed her food.

They'd ask. She knew they would. But she wouldn't tell. That he was gone. They didn't really want to know anyway.

"The past is over-" Danise muttered on autopilot.

The chair she was on may as well have been a life raft out in the middle of troubled waters. "You gotta treat it like it's over."

**chapter eleven**

Anukai heard the water against her skin before it registered that she was in it.

She opened her eyes and looked at the strange copper grate between her feet that it drained away through.

"I want to take you somewhere. Introduce you to some people. Take your mind off of all this. Put this in your hair and you'll get in."

Kahn reached through the falling water and gave her a tiny purple orchid. She squinted in shock.  He raised a finger to his lips and shushed her, then playfully pushed his face all the way through the veil.

"Don't worry, it's me. I know it's been a long time." he chuckled. " If it's not me, you won't get in."

They looked at each other, both silently amazed at how he seemed to have gotten younger in direct relation to her growing up.

Kahn shook his head in chagrin. "And wear something that shows off all  of that."he laughed. "It'll make it even easier."
"How am I going to know where to go?" she started.
"Wake up and I'll tell you-" Kahn the younger growled.


Anukai woke up with a start, wet sheets twisted around her in the fetal position. She looked down, alarmed.

A pale purple orchid was grasped in her hand.

She suddenly heard the echo of running water down the hall and jumped up.  She ran as heavy pressure slowed her.

When she arrived at the bathroom door, it was locked. She soundlessly pounded on it for what felt like forever until it opened on its own.

Anukai stumbled over to the running shower and ripped open the curtain.

She found herself cowering in the far corner of the tub around another orchid crushed by the terror that gripped her as the droplets of hard water slammed into her head and face in slow motion.

'Ana is…ok?" Anukai wiped at the face of her fractured soul, quietly pleading with herself to snap out of it, for self to register to her self.

When the splinter of herself finally looked up, a soft, tentative smile spread across both aspects. She gingerly pulled herself out of the shower and turned it off. They blinked in unison.

**chapter twelve**

*Du-du...du-du-du...Du-Du-...du-du-du..*

Little Anais woke out of strange dreams so fast that the  forget me not flowers blossoming on her pillowcases as she slept were still dancing in her hair to music not playing outside of her yet.

But it was coming. She could tell by the heartbeat of the house. Today was going to be one of those days that Home was going to be just like Heaven.

Bass began to echo in the walls. It was about to start, she just knew it. She could tell before she could see it happening, just like always.  She hopped up, brushed some of the flowers out of her hair as she hurriedly made her bed and tore down the stairs like it was Christmas. When she got to the bottom landing she looked down. To wait for it, and feel it in her feet before she saw it. The heartbeat of the house was stronger the closer she'd gotten to its epicenter. Shyly, she looked up, little brown face flushed with adoration and excitement.

"HI DADDY!" she screamed across the cavernous living room. Her father looked up from the turntables in the corner of the room and beamed the bodacious blush-grin of his she'd asked for before being born back to her. It didn't have much furniture in it yet. But today, because it was that kind of day, the living room had crates of records everywhere. Anais soft-shoed through the veldt of possibly perfect music slowly, so as not to stub a toe.

"...Another party?" she yelped. He bent back over the vinyl already whirling on the players, his ear pressed to his left shoulder as he listened intently before he wove one sound into another. Her whole body bounced happily to the bass that began to shake the house basement to attic.

"Well ...this time, it's a wedding~" he grinned sheepishly at his child as she corkscrewed up in the air excitedly. "Wait-" he muttered stoically, trying his best to keep a straight face.

Anais followed suit and looked at him with the stoniest, most professional face she could make at the moment to prove she could handle crewing. "Alright! You can go! You can go!" he laughed. She jumped up in the air again then ran towards the kitchen, leaping over his wooden crates like a deer.

"...And get those flowers out of your hair, you know your moms would have a fit-" he called after her then flipped it.

You and I by Rick James flooded the house with light and music."Du-du...du-du-du...Du-Du-...du-du-du…I knew it," Anais sang confidently. "I just knew it." She yanked a chair from under the kitchen table, swung it to the cabinets and leapt up on it to the counter barefoot. The box of sugar smacks she had hidden behind the second box of nasty corn pops that her older brother always had to have was still there.

"You and me We are as close as three-part harmony Wouldn't you agree And if by chance Our romance ended it would surely be The end of me~" she sang happily as she hopped across the rim of the sink to grab her favorite  oversized coffee mug and spoon from the drying rack.

"Hey Anais," her big brother Fluke called out to her from the TV room around a mouthful of his third bowl of Saturday morning cartoons cereal. "Thanks for putting your grimy  toes near things I have to eat off of-"

"The things I do with you So far as I'm concerned They all can go to hell~" she sang loudly and stuck her tongue out at him crazily.

"She cussed!" he screamed like a stool pigeon, spitting cereal everywhere.

"I was singing!" she screamed back happily.
"Now sing it, sugah-" her father sang out with the record. Fluke rolled his eyes.

"Du-du...du-du-du...Du-Du-...du-du-du~ " Anais yelled as loud as her little lungs could, face shining like a flashbulb that had just gone off in a dark room.

"Kiss-up-" Fluke muttered and went back to pouring his fourth bowl of corn pops, emptying the box and utterly explaining why they always had to buy two of them whenever he was allowed to get them. Anais stood there quietly until he looked up. "What?" he grumbled. She tossed the backup box to him.

"…thanks." he grunted.
She rammed a spoonful of cereal into her mouth, crunched it and showed it to him, laughing maniacally.

"You're such a child," he muttered and went back into teenage Mutant Ninja Turtles, bouncing absently along with the house without realizing it.

She shrugged her shoulders and danced out of the room back towards the in-house deejay, in search of a specific crate that contained the album covers that answered everything she'd ever think to ask.

It was in the middle of the dining room, under the big oak dining table.  The blue, green and brown whirls of color in the carpet morphed to a marsh and the tigers she'd drawn all over one side of the crate and not gotten in trouble for  sprawled lazily alongside it, tails flicking absently to the beat.

She sloshed through the sudden wetness soaking her flannel pin-dotted nightgown and got down on her knees. Tiger cubs nuzzled her bare feet as she flicked through the vibrantly colored records one by one, a severe look on her face.

"Flick. Flick. Flick." she muttered as she raced through the albums like the child of a Deejay she was. She was the only one in the house allowed to even touch his records besides  him due to the professional flick of those fingers. "Jackpot!" she smiled and pulled out one that made all the difference in the world.

Anais scrambled from under the table and ran over to her dad, brandishing the colorful record like a demand instead of a request. She rolled her eyes as she waited for  him to look up in the midst of figuring out his basic set list. He looked up, ear still crunched to his shoulder like he was searching for signs of life in space and made a quick motion with his hand for her to pass it to him. She handed over the album, curtsied, and bounded up the stairs to brush her teeth as the strains of the song bled into what he was on now, which was always something gloriously  different than before.

Catapulting herself up onto the lip of the sink, she put twice as much toothpaste as she needed on her brush and turned on the water. Half was knocked off. She scrunched her face up, muttered "fine," then grinned broadly.

With each swoosh of the brush against her baby teeth she remembered the story of how he and her mother met and how it made total sense of what her guardian angel had told her about where she was actually from. Word upon word. Breath upon breath.

"Line upon line, God?" Anais whispered as she poked at her gums where two of her teeth hung on for dear life.

She felt God nod yes in the air around her, closed her eyes and somersaulted off the edge of the sink.

**chapter thirteen**

Roads he knew faded in and out of one another as he walked aimlessly in the cold. The longer Gabryl walked, the more he knew he wasn't the one who was insane.

"She's the one who's crazy! She's the one trying to act like she didn't do-" he seethed. The words tried to ram themselves back down his throat so as not to curse his own mother.

"It's not just me! It's what she put ALL of us through-" he cried out at the darkening sky, aggravated by his chest suddenly starting to itch. It reminded him of shit  he had damn near lost his mind defiantly refusing to recall.

Flashes of memories from being in the hospital as a kid flooded up and he bent over as if sucker-punched, lacerated all over again a good ten years after the fact.

"Ooh! Fuck her!" he groaned, winded by the brutality of his memories. "Fuck her!" he screamed, looking up at rundown brownstones on a block he couldn't place for the life of him.

'You tell'er, man!"a boy catcalled from a stoop he was near. "Yaass, bitch!"another drawled.

Gabryl looked up and saw he had inadvertently rolled up into Lost Boys territory, called that due to the scores of Alphabet kids kicked out of apartments all over the city that gravitated to the alternative lifestyles community center nearby and the underage trade that went down in the area under the cover of darkness, all the way over to the west side highway.

He squinted, realizing he knew some of them from detention.

"Which bitch we saying Fuck her to," one boy plainly asked, "though you know, a bitch is a bitch is a-"

Gabryl looked away.
"Ooh- I know that look- we all do-"
"It's his moms-"
"Oh, then Nigga, you's in good company here-"
"Word-"
"What she do? Throw you out?"

Gabryl grimaced angrily. She didn't but may as well have with her craziness.

A boy as slight as an eleven year old girl with the weary eyes of an 80 year old man sang out. "With nothing but the played, boring assed clothes on his back?! Tha- Whore-rah!"

"They do that shit allatime-"
"Yeah, fuck'em. If you need gear, holler here-"
"Brotherhood of the hoods-" the plain-speaking boy muttered.

Gabryl felt awkward for a minute as any alarm he may have felt evaporated. "Thanks," he said, coughing.

One of the Lost Boys lobbed a hoodie at his head. "In case it gets colder tonight," he said. "It always does." Gabryl tied it around his hips and thanked the kid again. "No worries. We got you. And always remember. If it gets too wet and cold-"

"There's always the club," a few sang out dramatically.
"Which club? And how much is it to-" Gabryl asked awkwardly.

"Any of'em around Chelsea. And with Jagger's gear and that innocent-assed face of yours, they ain't gone charge you shit-"

"Just don't go hopping into cars and shit-"
"Unless you…"
"Yeah, it's never worth it. Always goes sideways with the Pedo Purveyors. Male or Fem, Straight or Gay."

They hopped  up to leave but looked back at him staring stupidly at the ground.

"We were bout to head up over to Embryan anyway- you're obviously straight but thirsty as hell…but they like that- They'd feed us all for bringing your ass in."

Gabryl looked at the crowd of boys, completely confused. Plain-speak rolled his eyes. "Hungry?"he asked. Gabryl nodded stiffly.

'Come with us…and leave your Earth behind-" Jagger sang out the lyrics to a Chemical Brothers song they all knew.

"Bright and clear, we see the light- all universes at your side…Please lead us to other sun's warm light-"

"Behold, they're coming back…"the rest of the Lost Boys sang out, " Behold~ they're coming back… they're coming back-"

**chapter fourteen**

Anukai woke with a start, soaked sheets now dry. She looked over at the alarm clock, the orchid absently stuck behind her ear. It was 1:05 am. She dressed in the dark, knowing her mother was knocked out on the other side of the house.

She pulled on ripped black footless tights she had thrown into a corner earlier that night, then a bright red bra and a black fishnet body-suit before she put on a mini-kilt  and reached for shredded diy chaps that she always liked to wear with it. She slid into her oversized black hoodie  as she stepped into the black converse tennis shoes she loved to dance in  that looked like they smelled.

Anukai grabbed her first ever pair of black aviators and rammed them on. The orchid that had been tucked behind one ear fell. She looked at it, down at her outfit then rammed it between her breasts under  the hoodie and body-suit.

She gave a grown, *"don't mess with me"* scowl into the mirror then blushed like the sixteen-year old that she actually was in the dark, then looked around.

"Now what?" she thought to herself.

*"Meet me in the woods,"* she heard whispered in her inner ear. *"I got you from there."*

Anukai locked her door and pushed up the big window that opened onto the porch roof and  slid all the way out, scuttling down pine trees that hid her escape before she shot off down the block  in the cover of darkness towards the ravine.

**chapter fifteen**

On the other side of the dresser mirror, Gabryl sat huddled up against the wall in Anukai's bed.


He tried to think of sleep instead of who else she was hearing and running off to or where he was trying to be as far away from as possible in his own head by hiding out in bed with her.

**chapter sixteen**

That day's bitches and hoes whirled around her head with the sick beats she'd fought tooth and nail for the right to be in the booth with misogynistic fucks to create.

She popped the handful of benzos the aftermath of the gauntlet she created in demanded as she headed out of the door to the waiting car.

She settled in the cushy back seat. It was 1am. An early night.

She looked down with aggravation at the acrylic nail she'd ripped to the quick having to knock one of the abusive lackeys of the gang producing tracks that day off yet another under-aged girl smart enough to get off the street but not strong enough to make the beasts she'd run with stand down.

The younger the girls were, the more violent the cowards were to them in front of their boys.

Her nail had snapped when she'd pent him to the glass with her elbow and clawed him in the face.

She grumbled as the day reloaded across her in the back seat soon as she closed her eyes.

**chapter seventeen**

"Get the fuck outta my studio!" she roared over the lackey screaming as she head-butted him. She was ten times faster with her fists than any of the always inebriated, bloated bodyguards in the crew.

"Get that bitch, yo!"the main artist screeched in protest at the head producer from inside the recording booth.

Lead looked up at the egg-crated ceiling and sighed melodramatically, a sound that stopped all action but hers in the studio.

"Don't… call her a bitch-" he murmured. "She's the only reason you have a fucking song in the first place. And the one take I'm giving you and these fools-"

The bully angrily pushed through his boys who'd wedged between  him and the one everyone called Tee[short for Auntie], stopping  just outside of what he thought was her reach. Her nose flared as the cockiest grin of authority spread across her face.

"Don't try her, dude," the head producer warned the bully. "She's why you know who doesn't interview without sunglasses."

"What? I'm posed to be scared of this fugly bitch?!"he yelled, leaning back as she swung her fist towards his head.

It would've been perfectly gauged on his part if she hadn't opened it at the last moment and pimp slapped the other side of his face with that same heavy- assed hand she'd done the initial damage with. The little girl he'd attacked charged into the brawl and flung herself between the two of them.

The head producer dropped his head in his hands and stood up. The room froze. "Girl. Get up." Defiantly wild-eyed, the girl stood up.

"How old are you? Fourteen?"
"In a bit" the girl whispered.
"You're the one who wrote that poem, right?"
The kid nodded, shocked they'd even told him.

"Look- You wanna hang here…you gotta be willing to stab these motherfuckers when they roll up on you wrong- aight?" She nodded. "Go sit the fuck down-"

"You- You- You know the fuck who I'm- What the fuck does this motherfucker do in this creative enterprise of yours?" he said absently to the artist angrily pressed against the locked, glassed in booth.

"Um, um-" the rapper stammered.
"Get him the fuck outta here-" The producer said evenly. "And if anybody-"he added diffidently "Ever says anything to any of my people …about him rolling up on any kid, cut off his balls."

He looked around. "Everybody not contributing to the atmospheric motherfucking ecstasy  we're making up in here get the fuck out of my fucking studio!" Lead roared.

A third of the bodies present scurried out behind the disgruntled and wounded bully.

**chapter eighteen**

Anukai  veered away from traffic into the trees that led down into the ravine.

She groped along the concrete breakers strewn at the bottom that her and fellow ravine-rat heads had covered in obituary tags for those that could no longer run the race. She came to the one she had helped Adam plaster with spray-paint and tribal markings ahead of time.

She crouched down and ran her fingers across it. The unpainted sections of the makeshift tombstone gleamed white in the clear night. An oddly familiar voice called out.

"Now don't you go getting all sentimental on me-" Kahn the younger purred. "You, of all people, know he's not… you know, he's just… no longer here." Anukai dusted her hands off and stood up to face him.

"You look different."she murmured. It had been a long time but this was the first time he'd registered as beautiful, almost despotically so.

His arms were sinewy and shone like alabaster in the light of the moon, as did snippets of his flesh through the destroyed tee-shirt that hung off of him. The leather jeans he had on were studded down the sides, the aviators that he pushed up into his prematurely silver hair as reflective as the rest of him, revealing irises that were now the color of mercury.

"Younger. Like you've had the afterlife beat outta ya-" Anukai snickered.

"Har-har." he dead-panned. " And you …look older. Do you want a hug?" he asked awkwardly.

"No. I want him back." she whispered.

"You know he was miserable here, Anukai." Kahn replied gently. "Even damned, you know it's an improvement on what he had to put up with in this realm-"

"Is he in Hell?" she asked her old Guardian who now seemed too young in the face to guard anything at all.

"For all you know, you might be in Hell yourself right now." They both chuckled.  "Let me see your hand." Kahn murmured. He turned hers over in his.

"Sloppy," he laughed,"but at least he stopped you from wilding out right as he was out the door." They got quiet. " It's healing fast. How many stitches?"

"45." Anukai whispered absently and looked up at the sky.

"Let Us go." Kahn said simply.
"Where, exactly?" she muttered as she struggled out of the jean chaps and hoodie.

Kahn the Younger chuckled absently. "To your boy's going away party. Prearranged-"

Kahn wrapped around her like a cloak and slid his hand over her eyes. Anukai reached up and pried apart two of his obscenely long fingers, watching as her cells began to shatter under the compression of him as they literally exploded into the cover of  darkness together.

## chapter nineteen

The reverb made Tee grin, relax more into the back of the car as she drained the split of champagne always waiting for her in it. Because she remembered.

Lucky Lead had said and done something similar for her what felt like a lifetime ago. Defended her. Fended off a fuck that shouldn't have been trying to fuck with her young ass as it was, like the asshole could smell on her what she'd already fought her way through in her hood, hiding out  all those boroughs away.

Same way somebody else  had once  protected a vulnerable Lead. It was the only  thing you could do in a war like this. And the warriors who'd survived it all did it wordlessly for the ones like them they ran into.

All she wanted…needed at this point in time the way her days ran was release. A sense of wordless innocence to erase it all by holding her until she fell asleep.  That was why her driver took her across the river this way.

She was ripped out of her thoughts by her driver slamming on the breaks as the clouds burst open. Rain pounded into the skylight of the towncar as she drained the bottle in her hand . She laughed as the benzos kicked in and popped another chilled split out the roof of the on-call car. Her driver started and stopped again, tossing her around in the back as she tried to close the roof. A deja vu momentarily pinned her to the backseat as the rest of her body seemed to go on autopilot.

The window rolled down and the back door popped without her opening it.

**chapter twenty**

Gabryl shivered like the boy he still was against his will, huddled in a doorway a few buildings down from the club the Lost Boys had taken him into.

He blocked out what he had seen and deflected in the Embryan and pushed on, weirdly drawn back towards the river on the far side of the highway without recognizing it.

It was his now technically fourth night in the cold with nowhere else to go.

She'd been there before. Surely she'd show up again.

The first two nights she'd sized him up like the replenishments his energy would be to her, rolling through this zone. He'd looked away, angry, bewildered, waiting for his friend's mom to go work third shift so he could sneak in.

Right as he gave up the sky started to sputter rain down on him. Defeated, he stepped out into the street, instantly soaked to the bone. Bright lights slashed through the night and blinded him as the driver blared his horn and slammed on the breaks.

**chapter twenty one**

The driver beeped his horn again impatiently.

A scrawny, lanky kid with a shaved head stood in the middle of the road in a t-shirt, blinded by the headlights.

Irked, he rolled down his window and barked. "Kid! Stop covering your damn eyes and-"

"Stop high-beaming me!" Gabryl yelled back, drenched and shivering in the downpour. The driver sucked air through his teeth.

"Shut up and get in the car!" her driver roared.

Bewildered, Gabryl looked and saw the car door standing open in the downpour. He looked up at the clouds, tears running down his face hidden  in the rain. "Thanks,"he whispered to the sky  and dove into the towncar.

**chapter twenty two**

The woman momentarily nodded awake to the sound of water splashing in the sink before she went back under.

The reverb of a guy she didn't know who'd roughly grabbed her by the hair and pinned her to a wall for a crossroads kiss flashed in front of her eyes.

A biochem stamp of DBLHELIX on his tongue activated on contact with her spliced saliva. Her body pressed violently up against his as the element soaked her system like a hard rain.

"Enjoy the ride, baby," the unknown slurred, eyes wild by how quickly she'd crossed and made his presence unnecessary.  A shock of tenderness shot out from his eyes, startling her. The unknown flashed a confused smile full of the chaos he'd just kissed her with.

She blinked and he disappeared.

Her eyes fluttered.

Again she felt the tangle of limbs around her. The pulse of the place careened through the drenched and discarded DBLHELIX'd bodies strung out alongside her.

Strobe lights. Darkness.  Bass. Repeat.

Groans echoed from the tracks that spun in the  atmosphere and the bodies closest to her.  She tried to focus on the eyes of the "friends" she had in the crush.

An obscenely beautiful jaw here, bizarrely elongated leg there, Adaptives as well as Latents waiting for an Aware to bridge the gap for them, blindly faking it until they made it to a taste of whatever it was that made those like her glow so radioactively underground.

They were  loyal to the self-hatred woven through the entire Day-tripper dance, who got fucked up with her just to make sure she wouldn't get away more. They kept her under the guise of keeping her company.

Latents licked the Helix sweat off her and temporarily glowed in the half-light of the club, murmuring.

" ALL is GOOD…Perfectly alright to need a little help to break free," a British chick slurred against  her lip.

"We're…all in this together," meowed another as he gently bit down on the inside of her thigh, delirious.

"The connection you have is wild," a shaggy-haired girl with dilated eyes purred.

The woman didn't feel any of it. It was obvious from the deadness in her whited-out eyes that they were all too terrified to look into in the dark, even as they fed.

Like a bored beast who played with food that wished it could devour her instead, she laid there nipped by the nervous cruelty of each random caress, nuzzled with the panic that coursed through them, aware of nothing else other than she wasn't as ripe to be fed upon as she made herself look.

Awares like her who'd gotten fucked up just to escape the greatness pouring out of them awake in a hellish world lived like marked men and women during the day.

By night they were scattered across the Bunker in their respective piles of Latents and Posers allowing their sweat to be fed upon, for things to be licked and rubbed that remained numb no matter what.  They pretended as best as they could that the distraction was working in case any of other Aware brethren would see the  futility in the farce tattooed across their faces, outting them for not being able to be literally "down."

"I wonder what it would be like with an Other instead?" she mused to herself, looking at an Aware across the way.

She bit down on the strange lines on the inside of her jaw to make more of the drug release into her system, engineered smack that the wild-eyed unknown bodhi in attendance had given her, receipt of which was not normally her style.

Whatever it was…it was good. It out numbed the numb.

Her body arched and the mouths of those kneading at various pockets of her gasped as it instantly passed through their membranes  and slurred visions already whirling in front of their eyes due to her.

She grabbed the head resting on her inner thigh and gently shoved him off into a crumpled heap on the floor, suddenly needing to pee. As she absently rose up her eyes fluttered again.

**chapter twenty three**

Roughly his life ran over him like a fucked up movie as Gabryl curled up on the sofa.

The home of  some 35 year old chick who apparently had thought he was cute enough to screw out in the rain spun feverishly around him. She  had taken him all the way out to Jersey. He had no clue how he'd get back, but at least he was inside.

His head and chest were covered with vapor-rub she gave him to try and break the fever she could tell he  had before he'd even flinched away from her fingers reaching for his forehead.

With every blink on the couch he hurtled back and forth between the smell of menthol, the  strangely plush couch he was on, and Anukai's white room that he couldn't help but see as yellow with the strange slatted window across the way that meant something to him that he couldn't understand no matter how hard he tried.

Even in his head her room made his skin crawl without her in it. He tried to shake it off yet remain still enough to stay patched into her bed so he could sleep with the smell of her in peace, wrapped in her scent in the sheets. Frustrated, he looked up at the ceiling.

The Lost Boys had been right about the Embryan welcoming him like the fresh meat he looked like to their clientele. More right than they'd realized.

Free drinks had rained down on them like they'd just returned from the hunt but he'd only fucked with the food and clocked what the fuck they'd taken him into for refuge. Some of the men couldn't be bothered  with their obviously young asses. Others stood so engrossed by the go-go dancers soaping each other up on the raised platform in the middle of the dance floor that a car crashing through the bar wouldn't have gotten their attention. But it was watching men obviously two and three times their age circle them like sharks that had got his hackles up.

The Lost Boys were so in their element that only Plain-speak noticed when Gabryl wandered off looking for the bathroom.  He had crashed into him when Gabryl had stopped suddenly at the banquet of an old, dirty chicken queen glowing darkly in the folds of the space, surrounded by thugged out black boys kiki-ing like crows.

"Banjee Boys," Plain-Speak muttered. "Aggressive bottoms to the bone, worshipping that white devil throne, like literally-" he chuckled. "Bathroom, right?Come on-" he wedged past him as Gabryl kept standing there, trying to place the face of the man in the middle of the crush pouring drinks for all the young boys at the table until they overflowed.

All laughter at the table screeched to a halt as the man recognized Gabryl mid-pour and all the color drained from his face. The pallor change was what had jogged Gabryl's memory.

He stood there as his bewilderment shifted to rage. His fist balled up as his mother's rapist shriveled in the banquet. It had been the first time either had seen each other since his Grandpere's funeral.

Gabryl had shoved his way out the crowd onto the street  and had run down the block before getting soaked and spirited away to fucking Jersey.

He was racked with empathy for long lost Danise against his will as he angrily cried, trying to sleep.

He finally gave up, let himself out and headed back to the city.

**chapter twenty four**

"Anukai! Get your ass down here and clean up this mess you made before you go to school!"

Anukai squinted her eyes shut, trying to go back to her strange dreams.

"NOW!!" her mother barked. A litany of abuse followed, words spewed so roughly that even her mother screeched to a halt in shock. She glanced at herself in the mirror over the blocked hearth in disbelief. Her fists were clenched and teeth bared as if mid-battle with the stalking ex-husband she'd served papers to camped up the block with his latest accomplice instead of yelling at her teenaged daughter.

The beast camped out in the mother's shadow smirked at her returning to form so easily.  It sinisterly slunk alongside her and whispered as her mind flooded with memories of Anukai losing pints of blood due to a gash on her hand. The few weeks between then and now felt like lifetimes.

At best, Anukai reminded her of all the things she hated having given up on within herself. At worst she called up vengeance the mother would never direct to the man who truly deserved it.

That she could still see puddles of blood on the TV room floor when she tilted her head the way she'd forgotten she could didn't matter.  Neither did the fact that she knew that the garbage all over the kitchen was left by Anukai's freed from the spectrum, perfectly  maladjusted, pubescent younger sister, Flower, to get back at her for refusing to let her borrow jeans the night before.

The despair that had recently shaken her mother in a pool of blood was replaced by old rage.

Their truce was obliterated by a few seconds of inner-talk as the guardian of the mother switched streams for its own entertainment.

*"There is no peace for the wicked. That's biblical, even. And You've always known SHE is wicked. So give her NO peace."*

The mother self-righteously snarled in the mirror  and stormed up the stairs to battle at a little before five to seven in the morn.

**chapter twenty five**

The water from the faucet sounded much farther away than was possible unless she was suddenly ten feet tall.

"Like Alice," she chuckled crazily to herself.

She couldn't feel her hips, only knew that they were pressed awkwardly up against the sink and that it was hard to come up from whatever was in what she had blindly taken to go under. She tried to get her throat muscles to swallow.

Her eyes did their best to focus on her reflection in the mirror but something was wrong. The image was too pulled together, too sleek to be her.

She angrily looked away and raked her hand roughly through the wild hair she knew that she had left the house with, hair that what was in the mirror had yanked back severely. The eyes in  the mirror image didn't budge as its body mimicked the motions of the woman living the lie outside of it, one beat behind.

Trying her best to hold onto the last snatches of french-kissed incoherence she'd plastered up in the front of her brain, she narrowed her eyes at her sober self in the mirror.

Her Ka mimicked her as its hair slowly unfurled to match the mane on the other side of the looking glass before it slicked back of its own accord again. The Ka looked away.

Her ears popped and the sound of rushing water erupted.

"I know that shit wasn't that strong-" she muttered abrasively and lurched down to splash water on her face. Her reflection remained erect, a snarl spreading with each splash of water.

Visibly on edge, the wet faced woman stood back up. Her mirror image stood stock still, defiant and dry as a bone, eyes narrowed.  Suddenly her reflected Self rose up  through the mirror and slapped the shit out of her.

She fell to the floor in a shower of glass. Blood spilled out of her lip as she looked up at herself, bewildered.  "What the-" she choked.

"This is what happens when you take shit from strangers!" her Ka snarled as she crawled out the mirror and loomed over her lesser Self sprawled on the floor trying to scream.

"What?!" her Ka screamed, "You think you're just going to be able to drug this shit away?! You think you can just go to your morbidly pathetic, psuedo- happy place after you just so glibly set me free?!" her Ka roared. "Oh you've clearly forgotten what the fuck  you are-" it seethed.

"But-but I-" the woman stammered, cowering.
"Shut up!" her Ka screamed,"You fucking ruptured me with this bullshit!" she yelled and locked the door her lesser Self had been too high to latch when she'd entered. "And to Hide here?! Of All Places? With your *friends*?!" she howled.

She couldn't even look at herself. "THEY **hate** you! More than you hate yourself! That's why they're here! They only get a taste  of what you have naturally flowing through you sniveling in your sweat! You have what they want, what they'd give anything for and can't get- and- And look at you!!"

"I didn't ask for this!" The woman screamed.
"You've burnt half our mainframe out! You don't know what the fuck you asked for!" her Ka roared.

"They get fucked up with you Literally for the residuals of life in the taste of what you excrete.  They're  fucking spiritual coprophiliacs! That's all this is- to stretch this fucked up moment out longer and longer with you locked up in it  instead of just breaking free-"

"They-they're my friends!" The woman whimpered.
"Great! Now you sound like that fucking mother you got cursed with-" her Ka seethed. "They were your friends? Then why didn't you call ANY of them on the day You chose to die?!' she roared.

The woman laid there bleeding and speechless.

"Exactly." her Ka snarled.  "They say you'll all get clean together, but they won't because you clean cannot be here with them ! And YOU know it!" The Ka looked around the bathroom in disgust. "And Yet this is- THIS is where you hide!"

The woman continued to stammer inside of her head, begging her body to move.

"Who do you think you're telling to move, Baby?" her Ka asked. "Who are you begging? Don't you get it? Don't you see? Did the bullet do That much damage?" she whispered.

"Bullet-?" The woman choked.
"YES!The BULLET!" her Ka snarled, turned  around and tossed it into her own lap.

"I'm-The soul you've been hell-bent on breaking-I'm What

fucking makes you move- How the fuck are you gonna move without me?" she hissed, then paused."But I'm not who is doing this to you, Art-"

The woman's eyes slammed shut at the start of the  name she wasn't ready to hear."That-that's not My name- my name isn't- that's not me! It's-I'm- " she gasped, suddenly shaken by the sight of her own blood seeping through the lacerations on her arms from the broken mirror.

Her Ka sighed. "You're right. You're not-you can't be who you're called to be- until you quit doing this...and If you make me burn it out of you, I will." she growled. "Just like I promised all those lifetimes ago."  Something inside of the woman on the floor shifted at the threat. She silently rose up and cracked the muscles in her neck like a boxer.

"Then be ready to burn this whole motherfucker down, because I will Never be That !" the woman growled and threw her Ka back against the broken mirror, pinning her against the shards of it by the throat until, slowly but surely, the bloodied pieces of broken glass on the floor and in the numb flesh of her arms floated back up into place and sealed her sense of Higher Self in the bloody yet resituated mirror in a haze.

"THIS is what you choose to remember how to do?" her Ka seethed. "All right. So Be It. But THIS time-It's MY version of this shit!" the Ka roared. The woman refusing to be named cupped her ear to the glass and played deaf. She turned off the tap with a malevolent smile, gave the middle finger to herself in the mirror, threw the door open and sauntered back out into the club, eyes fluttering again.

"Fuck you? Oh! Okay- Like I said...**So Be** It." her reflection whispered as the door swung shut.

**chapter twenty six**

An almost old enough to be gone Anukai remained militantly rigid under piles of comforters. She poked a bleary eye out to check the time.  "6:58" she muttered to herself, enraged.

"Ignore it," suddenly cut across her senses so strongly that she gasped.

He slammed his hand over her mouth in the spirit to muzzle her in the dark heat of the cocoon of blankets they'd been dreaming in, back to back, thousands of miles apart.
"She has to leave by seven no matter what, remember?"

She struggled from under his grasp. "And YOU are not supposed to even be here anymore, Gabryl" she seethed  in the spirit.

"Whatever," Gabryl hissed back, "If I can't sleep here, I'm coming there, dammit-and you can't fucking stop me so shut up and go the fuck back to sleep!"

"6:59!" called out one of the Ones camped around her bed, its spiritual ear pressed up against the door as it shook, the mother getting closer and closer to contact.

Her eyes angrily fluttered against her will.

**chapter twenty seven**

In Gabryl's world, the banging on the door had already begun.

"Yo Gabryl, wake up- you got to get out of here before my mom comes home from third shift-"

The weary Angels that surrounded him asleep on his friend's bathroom floor tried to rouse him as quietly as possible from wherever he really was.

"YOU are not real and you need to leave me the fuck alone-" Anukai barked at him so roughly inside of herself that it may as well have come from the mouth of the mother stampeding towards her.

"Yeah? Well you ain't real either, and I'm still there, so there- and f-nah, I ain't even going to cuss back at you, fuck that-"

The Angels encamped around them on both sides of the mirror sprang up ready to fight.

"Children- "

The one her spiritual lisp still had her calling Thy-Thy grumbled softly on the battle line his two unofficial charges drew day after day, only to erase night after night within the wails of insomnia.

His tone made them both stop as the clock ticked all the way over to seven right as the mother slammed her hand down on the knob of the locked door.

"Sonafabitch! You evil little- you locked the door?! You are just like your fucking father down the road!" her mother screamed.

The clock radio in Anukai's room flipped on and announced the time and the state of rush hour  traffic already riled up on the road.  "I'm taking the fucking door off the hinges when I get home!" she cursed and ran down the stairs.

Within thirty seconds, she was gone, peeling down the street, finally focused on being on time for the review that was waiting for her at a job where everything was stacked against her.

About a minute later, Anukai sat straight up in her bed, eyes closed long enough for everything that wasn't supposed to be there to go away. Gabryl waited so she could see the hurt look in his eyes. Angrily, he grabbed her by the hair and kissed her on the forehead roughly, refusing to let her go. The smell of peanut butter flooded her senses as she sunk into the spirit of him but he faded away too quickly for it to even register to him that she had acquiesced.

When she looked around it was just her, those encamped and the God that had locked her into what this twisted life hers was amounting to, a God that none of those involved seem to have any real pull with.

"Stop looking at me like that~" she grumbled as One smiled softly and pointed at her alarm clock.  She looked.
Time was still frozen at 7:01 am.

"Thank you," Anukai yowled and slumped back down, kicking around until she was comfortable enough to fall back asleep.

"Go check on the boy," Comptroller Vayo Kahn Diaz muttered to himself as he dragged a rough hand across his forehead to try and stop it from throbbing.

The already on-edge guardian angel did his best to keep himself spiritually together under the brunt of two teenaged charges hell-bent on wilding out and not playing according to plan.

"This is why I didn't have kids-"

*"No it's not,"* One mumbled softly.

VayoKahn Diaz looked around the room warily.

*"Make sure he goes in to the school this time."*

If he had actually had skin on this plane it would have crawled.

 Kahn shook it off and disappeared in the shafts of light that bounced around the edge of the blinds.

**chapter twenty eight**

One peered down into her face as motions were made to call forth the aspects of herself already collected.

Bits and pieces of the young girl who still slept with her eyes open clustered around her daybed, the looks of concern on their faces mirroring what beamed out of One.

As if the aspects of her spirit still splattered within her flesh could sense the focus, she angrily flopped in her sleep before sighing harshly.

"She looks so uncomfortable," one of the little ones sighed. "How much longer does she have to stay here?" said another. "Not much longer," One intimated.

"Her guardian is going crazy," muttered one of the older ones. "But that's for other reasons," pointed out another.
 "…besides, his hands are full-"
"She's getting worse-and that other one? What the hell… is his-his-problem?" stuttered one through teeth that chattered as if she was always freezing, no matter how indifferent to heat spiritual bodies were supposed to be.

"She's fine, she'll be okay," piped in the littlest one around the thumb that she eternally refused to remove from her mouth.

"Yeah, she just needs to rest- can you make her rest-just for a little while?" the second to the smallest one called the twin said to the One that made everything possible in the first place, face turned up towards One expectantly.

"I've given her rest," One mused, "but maybe you all can make her take it."

Twelve aspects of Anukai leaned in a little bit closer to her, each sending her their clearest thoughts about the best parts of her life that they'd already had.

They encouraged her to keep on, tickling the rims of her eyes with things she had forgotten about so much that she started to chuckle in her sleep and swat at them like flies. She finally closed her eyelids all the way and they all sighed with relief.

"Not yet," One and the one with her thumb in her mouth hissed in unison as she held up her free hand to get them to stop.

She looked up at One, who nodded. Slowly she pulled her thumb out of her mouth for the first time in forever.

The rest of her crew gasped, each one slamming a hand over the mouth of the one nearest to them as she held a tiny finger on her right hand up to shush them.

Her drool soaked thumb danced over Anukai's forehead. Spit pooled on its tip like glycerin about to drop. "More than rest," the littlest one said stoically. "Heaven. Give her Heaven."

Everyone held their breath but the One. The smile of the proudest parent possible splayed itself across One's cheeks as the spittle began to drop towards its target.

Upon contact with the flesh that housed Anukai's third eye kinetic explosions burst across metaphysical layers and burnt all things instantly to black.

## chapter twenty nine

When the feet of Anais landed, they were on pavement wet after rain, sparkling with reflected light she couldn't see yet because her eyes were still closed.

She was pressed shoulder to shoulder with little cherubs like she used to be, all of them quietly bopping to the bass line shaking the air around them, waiting for her and One to teach them how to become all over again.

"Is she ready yet?" a little girl whispered in a flounced butterfly collar shirt and tiny shiny pants.
"Don't think so, her eyes are still closed-" whispered another.
"Anais, open your eyes!" the little girl called.
"Yeah, open 'em-" tiny Others chimed in melodically.
"Show us how-"

Anais laughed. Her toes tingled due to the good vibrations of her cherubic friends that aimed to ride the same wave as her. God gently squeezed her hand to say it was time. She opened her eyes and the Mad Hatter shone like the sun against a wet, hot, navy blue night sky over Cleveland. The cherubs gasped as if they hadn't been able to fully see their initial point of entry until they felt her spirit soar after she did.

Across the way, Bigs in their finest silks, satins and polyesters sashayed their way from polished yet beat-up rides to their weekly Xanadu, Soul Train-Soul Mate Saturdays at the Mad Hatter, the"Sho-Nuff BEST 'Bout to Be Baby-Making party in town, for all those wantin' to get DOWN!"

Anais scanned the crowd, searching for either one of them.

She saw her first.

The silk of the Halston dress pattern the woman had rubbed off from a grainy newspaper picture hung onto her barely there curves for dear life, screaming *Have Mercy* like the trail of men sprawled  in her wake dying over not even receiving so much as a glance through the roller-set that suggestively danced over one of her eyes like Lana Turner.

"There she is-" Anais said confidently.

"How do you know?" a pair of cherubs asked earnestly in unison as the woman wound her hips past another crowd of lovesick brohams in loud shirts tucked in and unbuttoned down to their tight velvet and polyester pants. The growls and purrs in her direction built up to a crescendo of cat-calls as she neared the first set of velvet ropes around the club.

"Listen," Anais instructed, then pointed to the men as they really began to howl.
"Hey Mama~"
"Please, Mama-Mama-Please-Please? Please?!"
"Mama, I'd sop you up with a-"
"Mama! Baby, Please! Mama you know Ain't nobody as bad as-"

"See?" Anais shrugged.
"Ohhh~" the cherubs around her whispered and nodded.
"But how are we supposed to know our Him-"a little cherub whispered shyly.

"Heeey, Daddy~" a cluster of scantily clad females sang out.

The entire crowd of cherubs whipped around and saw all six foot four of her him Saturday night strutting towards the door.

The mother and father of "Remembering what it was like being about to be" Anais met face to face after years of running on the outskirts of each other's circles as the velvet rope dropped to let their cluster of VIPs in.

"You sure?" God murmured to Anais.

In reply, Anais shot across the wet road like a bolt of lightning and grabbed both of their hands in the spirit.

The electricity of her so badly wanting to be coursed through the both of them. They looked at each other and their jaws dropped as the crowd of revelers carried them into the Mad Hatter to the sounds of the start of Car Wash.

The cherubs still clustered around God looked up at him expectantly. He smiled. They in turn scanned the perimeter and roared into the crowds in search of those destined to be their parents too, aiming to do their best to make it so their wave would also get "There" on time because there was so much work to do.

God shook his head and laughed before sliding into the haze around the neon lights.

**chapter thirty**

Anais did her best to hold onto both of their hands in the riptide of bodies but lost hold of Mama's hand like she always did in the remembering when the woman's "friends" descended upon her.

She stuck close to Daddy, who gave the nod to his Brothers as he made his way over to the main bar and got handed a Genny, gratis. The cluster of them surveyed the lush underground arena spread out before them like the professional  predators they were.

Along the upper perimeter of the club ornately carved tables fit for kings were positioned in front of vivid jungle murals newly created each Saturday morn after Fridays to be somewhat dry in time for the bodies pressed against them during wildest party in the city every weekend.

Beautiful Ones of both sexes attending the Madly Hatted VIPs wore wisps of animal skins, oblivious to the throngs of little spirit children that danced happily atop the tables, coyly making hedonistic connections between the ones they'd decided would most effectively get them to Earth on time.

The tables were piled high with feasts fit for a decadent Nubian nobility intent on making this night last forever, surrounded by every kind of throne the Art Director for the club who day-tripped designing sets for Karamu House could come up with. His worlds set off dance battles for the newest throne each and every week, stylized crowns, masks and crazy hats placed gingerly on each open cushion. Saturday set the stage for the wildest coronations ever seen, to the glory of the Pharaohs that throbbed in the blood and bones of all of those in attendance, satiating divine appetites repressed within them all, unfurled once a week at the Mad Hatter. Every conceivable kingdom these offspring of ousted and kidnapped peoples could imagine came to life for revelries whose flashbacks would get their hearts through the next week.

A few steps below the feasting VIP platforms was the DJ booth.  Clusters of cages arranged at the cardinal points of the dance floor were full of Beauties going off to the rhythm slamming through the speakers beneath them, wrapped in barely there zebra print bikinis. Sweaty bodies danced hard and long against each other in the pit below.

Daddy clocked the crowd like a villain 'bout to make a killin,' noting the sloppy Mixmaster techniques of the dude up before him as the guy bumped too much with his DJ booth hoes and made what should've been a simple Car Wash glide into Boogie Wonderland a hot mess. He and his crew gritted their teeth as the record scratched. The crowd cussed DJ Dude like it was nowhere near the first time that had happened. "What the hell-" both Daddy and Anais said at the same time, her cheek pressed to his hip, bony little spirit arms casually knotted around his thigh.

"Man- that shit's been going on all night-" One of his brothers that was actually related seethed when the record skipped again. "At least you know they'll be ready for ya-" he laughed.

"Duck, go get my weaponry-" Daddy chuckled absently to his cousin he paid to bring in his vinyl to parties.

"I already-" Duck hissed, inhaling as if there was twice the weed in the blunt lit between his lips than there was, "Did, maaaaan-!" On his exhale Duck laughed like the Disney character he'd gotten his nickname from.

"What do you mean you already-" Daddy started.
"That's your Earth, Wind & Fire, Daddy-" Anais whispered.
"That's MY Earth, Wind & Fire?!" Daddy yelled as if he'd heard her and shoved his cousin.

"Duck's 'bout to be goosed-" snorted one of Daddy's brothers before he took a hit and busted out laughing. Her Dad took off into the crowd, Anais on his heels, bobbing and weaving between bodies. She saw Mama with a cluster of girlfriends about to be zipped past by Daddy like she always did so she flung her spiritual body forward through the air to stop him.

He stopped short like he could see the little girl's body in a crumpled heap on the floor looking up expectantly at him like he always did. Anais shook off the stun, knowing she was being "seen" for the first time all over again, and roughly cocked her head in the direction of Mama.

Daddy's red-black skin gleamed in the half-light of the space as he was face to face with Mama for the second time that night. He grinned, a brilliant, unearthly smile that shone like the sun, so strong that even Mama's girlfriends were shocked into silence as she cockily brushed the hair out of her magnetic doe eyes, set to hypnotize even as she swooned from the sight of the perfect teeth housed in this beautiful pitch black man confidently blushing in the dark.

"What's your name?" Daddy grinned goofily.
"It's-" Mama began.
"Mama, NO!" an offended Broham nearby yelled so Anais couldn't hear her say her name.
"And yours?" Mama laughed.
"It's-" he started as his DJ Booth holding pen go-go's showed up.

"Hey Daddy, you ready?" they cooed in unison, some a few beats behind the others for effect.

They sized Mama up as not thick enough to be bothered by right as DJ booth dude scratched all over Daddy's record like he had lost his damn mind.

"Sonafa-" Daddy roared, sparks shooting from his eyes as his brothers pressed past him, smacking him on the shoulders and ass like this was football.

"We got this-you do.. You, maaan-" Duck crowed over his shoulder, sizing up Mama appreciatively as the Brothers and Cousins headed over to bring early DJ Dude's set to a close.

The music stopped abruptly and the entire club let out a cheer as Mixmaster SuckaDJ was forcibly made to back away from the turntables. Mama, Daddy and Anais noticed none of this.

"So…you dance?" Daddy asked Mama, Anais mouthing every word along with him.

"I was trying to, but he was killing me-" Mama laughed. Anais whispered word for word with her too, down to the giggle.

"Then…Don't worry-" Daddy whispered.  The crowd booed as the ejected DJ tried to get back in the booth so he could grab the few albums he'd shown up with, blocking the sound of Daddy saying Mama's actual name from the ears of preternatural Anais again. "If you Dance~I got you-" he growled, grinned and pointed from his chest to the booth, then to her.

Mama's girls fussed amongst themselves in disbelief at the one they called the Black Panther suddenly having eyes for the scrawniest of them all, even with the voluptuousness on display around her.

Amongst his go-go dancers the one with the buffalo penny nose got so indignant that she stomped away, rolling her eyes over the panther that had once been her Shaft obviously being sprung over bony Ms. Mahogany for all to see.

"You ain't got me yet-" Mama laughed, "but let's see if you can make me move, ain't gotta do much to be better than-"

"Scuse Me!" Daddy pardoned himself gallantly, leaving Anais with Mama to run  up the stairs to the booth.

 Mixmaster SuckaDJ pulled all 5'6" of himself up like he was going to have something to say 'eye to eye' with the father of Anais who was just shy of a full foot taller than him even without the platform boots all of them were wearing.

"Give IT to me-" Daddy growled and yanked two albums  of his stuck between SuckaDJ's three out of the guy's hand.

"How did you know I-"
"Man, please-" Daddy grumbled as his linebacker brother helped DJ down the stairs the old-fashioned way. Daddy slid behind the controls and blushed like he'd settled into a lush sports-car.

"Flip it, Daddy-" Anais whispered as Mama climbed up into a cage vacated by some of the dancers and folded her arms across her décolletage like she was waiting on him, back turned. Anais clamored into the pen with her.

All five of the brothers and his cousin, ringed by his pen of beautiful girls for effect took their positions in front of the booth like the secret service as bass flooded the place and hips began to move.

The crowd had no clue where he was going to take it but they all knew ahead of time that he was going to make up for all they'd suffered through leading up to his set.

"Do-Bop-Do-Bop-" she whispered. Anais bounced up and down as if she knew the song ahead of time like she always did. Daddy started weaving layers of sound into the hot and sweaty air like a refreshing breeze.

Instantly Mama forgot all about Daddy and lost herself in Dancing Machine mixed with a slightly sped up Donna Summer's Love to Love you, Baby resetting the groove.

Anais looked up in shock then danced in the spirit around her prancing one day gonna be Mama, only remembering to wave at Daddy when the horns broke out before the chorus. She giggled as him and all her soon to be uncles raised their left hands in the air out to the side and their right hands up to their ears, fanning the flames and rocking to the beat before switching to the other side as the go-go girls ringing the booth like fire wilded out.

Anais swore her Daddy could see the Love that was her dancing around Mama gyrating in ways she'd never own up to in the daytime, which was really what had all the fellas in the club hollering variations of "Mama! Damn!" in the first place.

She may have gotten teased her entire life for being too black, too tall, and too skinny in relation to everybody else, but her raw honey colored ass could Dance, with a capital D.

"Ladadadee-Ladadadadadada~" Anais sang, satisfied with the remembering as she floated over towards the man who really did become her daddy, surveying the hook-ups the other cherubs had learned to facilitate watching her recall.

The crowd exploded, everybody vibrating off of each other. Little spirit kids stomped through sweets on tables to the beats as their potential conduits and portals  started getting down.

Daddy took his eyes off Mama once only to switch albums and glance over at the little Angel that was the only one he had ever allowed in his booth as she broke into the same dance moves his brothers and cousins had practiced since they had been about the size that she looked in the spirit.

Then the next mash-up ricocheted across his brain and he was off, galloping after music to collage into sounds only previously heard in his  head.

## chapter thirty one

Vayo Kahn Diaz stood on the other side of the bathroom door massaging the bony spot above the cartilage in his nose. He was seething in a spiritual sea of Others also ticked off at what had become a daily dance with the splintered-off boy, the shielded one recalled as Gabryl.

"Go to school," Vayo Kahn hissed softly. The translucent aspect of his skin was ashen with anger as he did his best not to reach through the wall and yank the splice up.

"GO. TO. SCHOOL." he barked into the air compressed between the two walls, making the insides of the entire building shake. "That's it-" Comptroller Diaz yelled, slamming his fists into each other as Gabryl sheepishly turned the knob and passed an inch from the nose of the pissed-off guardian angel. An angry, nervous smirk was on his face until the frigid breath of the being bothered the wiry teenage boy's eyes. His friend called his name at the same time that Kahn came closer and he jumped almost out of his skin.

"Cool-come on man, let's go- you are cutting it too close with this shit- Don't get me th-th-thrown out too-" Byblos stuttered.

Byblos looked at one of his only childhood friends from the block that was still alive standing there in the same big black army boots, fatigues, hoodie and washed out, threadbare, shapeless black t-shirt that he'd shown up in after spending half the night out in Jersey, of all places.

"I can't b-be late. Here," he said, tossing Gabryl a brand new shearling coat given to Byblos for his birthday a few weeks ago.

Gabryl looked at him as if he'd never seen a coat before in his life.  His friend grabbed another coat out the closet. "What? It's cold outside," he said defensively, "and besides, it was too small for me when moms got it- just- just wear the da- damn coat, man- Let's go!"

Heads down, the boys made their way onto the block in silence. Somebody was already blasting slick rick's bedtime stories from a seedy fifth floor apartment as the streets woke up ready to out-do the drama of the words that lilted through the air.

They got to the corner where they always parted ways whenever Gabryl had been unable to bear his mom's sanctified hi-jinks. But this time Byblos felt like he was looking at his friend's face for the last time. Stuff had been wrong for a while but something in his eyes just looked like he was about to give up. Or explode. And either way, it  would be the end of the quiet dude who'd always just wanted to watch what was going down without being noticed.

"Yo, g-Gabryl-" Byblos asked hesitantly, bringing the boy's attention back to planet earth with a thud. "...you Aight?"

Gabryl's features tried to pull into a smile as he thought he nodded like nothing was wrong and walked away.  To Byblos, Gabryl's face hadn't changed at all. It looked like he hadn't heard a word.

"Haunted," Byblos whispered to himself, "...dude looks like he's haunted."   Byblos stood there thinking about a God he knew existed, even though he didn't bother with him very often. But right then and there Byblos started to pray.

"God, I- I don't know what's up, or what he's going through, and I don't remember much… except you love me- me, and you gave your life up for your friends…so please watch out for mines today. Even if you gotta use some of my angels from my momma to do it."

He instantly could hear his moms pitching a fit in the spirit soon as he'd said it. "Aight- Aight-" he sighed, "Please still keep enough watching me so I don't get shot either. Amen."

Byblos crossed the street and ran down the subway steps, muttering to a Mama who was scolding him in the spirit about Esau giving up his blessing for a bowl of rice.

*"Mama, it's not the same thing, I'm looking out for my boy like ya boy Jesus told us to do! Why do yall be twisting what it says like that? Dang!"* he fussed back at her in his head as he hopped on a train to go downtown to his magnet school.

**chapter thirty two**

Gabryl stomped through the neighborhood, his mind everywhere but where he walked.

Clusters of Ulterior Angels flashed out at him from whichever reflective surfaces he passed, standing like sentinels along his path.

Demonic so-called Guardians cowered comically on the sidelines whenever they thought his eyes might see them.

He defiantly ignored both groups.

Others that'd tied themselves to him after seeing his heart for Anukai filled out the rear while Vayo Kahn Diaz blended in with the morning crowds on the other side of the street.

Kahn looked off into the distance, nodded and then disappeared.

**chapter thirty three**

Anais kept staring at her baby teeth in the mirror.

Every once in a while she'd touch her tongue to the back of them, pushing them forward to make space for the big kid teeth she just knew were waiting in the wings of her gums.

"Give them time, Anais. They're coming. I promise you," God whispered into the top of her head through her weekend-wild tuft of ponytail hair. "Be patient, child."

She tilted her head to the side and pressed her tongue against the roof of her mouth. "Are they gonna be big?" she said in her head to the One who came up with the idea of her before she was even born. She felt him nod yes in the air around her. She narrowed her eyes a bit as she pressed him

"…How big are my teeth going to be?" she asked aloud accusingly.

"Big enough to make sense of that apple head you asked for! Or would you rather keep the baby teeth like a yuck mouth?" her big brother yelled, roaring with laughter as he sped past to use the bathroom, not even waiting for her to leave.  Anais rolled her eyes and stormed out to her bedroom, slamming the door behind her. "Stank-uuuuu!" Fluke called out sweetly after her.

She spent the rest of the morning playing with the hundreds of dolls that lived in her room. 427 dolls to be exact, ranging from four and a half inches to three feet tall, all efficiently named and numbered according to the plays and parts they'd won .

"There's a part for every actor, an actor for every part," she always reminded herself like she'd once read in a book on Hollywood and Babylon that she'd been too young to fully understand.

On Saturdays, every surface of her bedroom morphed into action, her very own MGM Grand studio lot. Plastic dolls and stuffed animals came from far and wide just for the chance to be a part of one of her stories, "some from as far as Taiwan," she whispered to God almost every Saturday without fail as she opened up the gates for business with either God or one of her Guardian Angels watching over her shoulder. Most of the actors on her sets with speaking roles were girls because outside of the perfume bottles-(the extras), He-man, GI Joe and a couple Ken dolls, most people gave her girl dolls.

Her cinematographer on most films was a burly fellow by the name of bear. Short for Cinebear. "He knows what I want it to look like without me even having to tell him" she murmured confidently.

The movies had a host of sound-stages and even occasionally went to off-site locations scattered around the house and yard. China was under the cherry tree back by the dogs, the jungle was under the various bushes her father grew around the perimeter, the kitchen sink was where they filmed all the swimming pool spectaculars, and the upstairs bathroom was the best location for all beach movies and anything that had to do with crowning kings and queens that was on the shooting schedule for the season.

It was a full-service studio: Movies, sitcoms, variety shows, even traveling stage productions sometimes.

The houses she built for the dolls to live in during the week flipped into additional sets for sitcoms of every shape and color on weekends. The dolls themselves were smart about the set-up too, renting out their homes to the dolls of friends who'd won speaking roles in movies shot by the studio whenever they were on location or when everything else went on hiatus and they went on vacation.

She looked at the clock. It was 1031 a.m. She was a minute late, which was bad because she demanded that everyone else be early.

"I have to set the example," she murmured to herself as she grabbed her wild hair, quickly braided two ponytails that hung down her back and then scrounged around  for her uniform as bear called out the various places it could be.

"Found it," she yelped. Still standing in her pajamas, Anais pulled on her red director's beret and the room shifted into action, picking up exactly where they'd left off.

She sat down cross-legged in front of a set she'd built from scratch, placing the appropriate actors on their marks as bear flipped through the clipboard of drawings she'd given him for the sequences they needed to wrap. Fuzzy stuffed animals waddled over to watch, waiting to be needed on-set with hands full of food grabbed from craft services.

Dolls with ornate hairstyles sat on top of lamps turned on their sides to light the scene about to be shot as others hung suspended by belts from the backs of chairs, drawing starry nights on backdrops that would be used later that weekend.

Every camera that entered  the house was at the disposal of bear and his crew. Four dolls moved two more into place around the edges of the homemade scrim, bringing the number up to 12 cameras for this one particular set of shots.

"I have to get all of it in one take, I don't think the actors can take doing it twice," she said to bear softly. He nodded and motioned for one more to be positioned to the far left.

God crouched down beside her, chin resting in his hands as he inspected how her animated toys got trying not to fidget the way they always did whenever he showed up.

"They know you're The money," she chirped when he asked about the sudden tension on-set. "You sign their checks!" she laughed. Today, all the dolls were naked except for strategically placed flesh colored Band-Aids.

"Why do the dolls have Band-Aids across their heads, chests and privates?" God asked casually, hiding his concern.

"That's wardrobe!" Anais sang out. "See-" she grabbed the little Glamour Girl named Dana and held her up for God to inspect. "I even colored the Band-Aids to make sure they were the same shade as them!" she said enthusiastically.

"Beautiful costumes," God murmured, "but where are we in the story?"  Behind him, bear rustled through some papers and passed the drawing to Anais, who was now up on her knees.

"They are wearing the Band-Aids because they all were hurt, but they survived, and now they're going to get healed. Well not right now, but-" Anais rambled on excitedly, "they know it now, that they will be  okay- they know things are different- they finally believe it. And because of that,  what hurt them  doesn't matter anymore-" she stopped shyly and sheepishly smiled up at him. "Right?" she whispered.

The reddish-brown irises of her almond-shaped eyes shook like they were defiantly holding on for life.

She waited for what felt  like an eternity for God to affirm what she'd always been told by nobody but him in their times together like this. God actually blush-grinned, furrowed his silvery brows in an attempt at seriousness, and gave a terse nod. The eyes of Anais went white with joy.

"Hm," God murmured. "I can't wait to see what you do next."

Anais stuck her chin out a little more, nodded confidently and was immediately sucked into the work of producing the movie at hand. There was a shuffle across the stage as Bear motioned.

Anais yelped "Action!"

## chapter thirty four

Little Anukai and Lil Gabryl stood in the wreckage of her church.  They'd tiptoed along the outskirts of the blackened scar on the ground where the art gallery rotunda used to be. He cried when she didn't until she finally let go and sobbed too.

Everything was in slow motion, but flooded by fast the way things do in dreams. They stood in front of the colorful scraps that were left of the stained glass windows and looked sideways at each other, not knowing what to say or to do for the longest time.

Little broken bodies of the killed off kids Gabryl had freed from nooses in the trees in her absence shuffled past to what had been the altar. They pressed hot faces against  what was left of the cool smooth stone as Anukai and Gabryl watched and silently continued to cry.

The only painting that had survived was the half-finished one of Gabryl. A group of lost boys had found it and had dragged it behind the nave for safe-keeping until she'd come back.

Little Anukai couldn't even look at it anymore. It had gotten wet and the face had blurred. The damage spooked Gabryl so much that he cried harder, angry tears that he couldn't explain. He knew he needed to say something about what else he was carrying around, but he couldn't for the longest time.

"...They killed my church..."Lil Anukai whispered when she could finally speak. Little Gabryl looked up from pushing patterns into the dirt with his toe in confusion. She looked okay.

"I heard the church was all of us, so that means you too, and you look fine." he said.

"What are you talking about? Look around-" she sobbed softly. "They broke everything!"

"But look at everyone who found it anyway!" Gabryl looked into the dirt smudged face of the kid closest to him and whipped the little blond boy around. The color was washed out of all of him except his eyes, which shone out of his head defiantly, like he'd gone through a war and won.

"They broke everything except what they really wanted to break-" Gabryl sang out suddenly, caught up so joyfully that Anukai leaned back in surprise.

"They couldn't touch what really mattered- you can build this again-you can paint and draw it all again and it'll all come back to life again, and-"

Anukai folded her arms over her chest and pouted. "I'll never draw again! They'll only come and try to destroy it! I don't want to play anymore."

Gabryl got in her face without saying a word. Anukai twisted up her lips all the more. "I will Never paint or draw anything again-" she growled. "I will NEVER-Ever!"

"Yeah you will." he said softly. "You got to-"
"Why?" she pouted angrily. His softness threw her off.

Finally he whispered it aloud. "I think I'm going to die."
"We all die." Anukai muttered.

"No, Anukai... I think somebody is going to try to kill me. Again. Not here, but-"

Anukai squinted her eyes against the red she suddenly saw. "If anybody wants to kill you, they're going to have to go through me!" she roared protectively.

The spirits of the beat-up kids around them cheered, roaring in ways  that made no sense coming out of their downtrodden bodies.

Little Gabryl smiled sheepishly. "See? That's why you-"

**chapter thirty five**

Kahn was at the foot of her bed, pensive at all he had seen in her as she slept. It took a minute to get her bearings as Gabryl's spirit faded as she woke. Shaken, a  teenaged Anukai woke up with a start.

"You know, you don't have to be so mean to him."

"It was just a dream" she muttered. "He's not real anyway-"
"Oh, but I am? Anukai, he's capable of being more real to you than I can ever-"

"Where is he then, Kahn? Where? You're here. I'm here- I'm awake, I'm not sleep anymore, yet you are still here." Anukai argued. "So what am I supposed to-"

"When was the last time you got a good sleep without waking up next to him?" Kahn interjected. She got quiet.  "Look, just because he's not Here doesn't mean he doesn't exist." Kahn murmured as he stroked his charge's sullen cheek. "Like me…but diff-"

"If this was Hell then he-" she yelped against strange thoughts that flooded her. Kahn brushed them absently away before they could even take root.

"But what if it's some kind of Heaven, Anukai?" Kahn whispered gently. "The fact that you've got me and everything else in spite of the hell that sometimes erupts around you- if this was Heaven- could you give me an inch and go… alright, it's possible that He… is out there somewhere… and can you imagine being nice to him?"

"But if that's possible, then it's possible I'd be able to find you too, right? Same logic, right?" she whispered.

He sighed, trying to side-step what he knew she was asking.

"Why do you need to find me? You know exactly where I am at all the time.  With you, preparing the road where you will be. Weaving myself into every aspect of it-"

"What if I don't want to take that road? What if I just want to be with you?" she cried out softly, sounding younger and older than she was at the same time.

"What other road is there?" he asked. "Be nice to him?"
"What does that even have to do with anything?" She fussed softly.

"You know what?" Kahn laughed accusingly "You may as well quit- I have known you since before your before- and I know how you are- if you didn't like him, he would have never been allowed to replace me over in that corner of yours- You like him! You're just scared."

"Scared of what?!" she yelped.
"Just… Scared! And we both know it! But you know what? that's not even the point! Right now, I command you-"

Her brows sliced up in shock at the word. Kahn glared right back at her and poked her in the center of her forehead where her third eye would open if she'd let it.  "That's right! I said I COMMAND you, dammit! BE nice to him-Other things bigger than your whiny "He's not real, so I'm going to be mean until he goes away because I can't afford to be crazy or get my hopes up about a God that would-"

"Alright." she seethed, cutting Kahn off so that he wouldn't finish that sentence.

"Good." he said sweetly. "Now get your ass up, get dressed and go pick up your things from "home" on the way to school."

Anukai looked around the room in search of something to wear. Bleary-eyed, her face twisted up into a scowl as she started to cry. "Something else bad IS going on, isn't it?" she sobbed, hugging her knees under the comforter.

"Yes," Kahn said curtly, refusing to put her at ease. "How can you tell?"

"Because I can't figure out what to wear!" Anukai sobbed. "Women," Kahn laughed at her and cleared his throat as he stepped to the side.

On the floor behind him Gabryl had thrown into a pile her combat boots, freshly laundered boy socks with navy blue rings at the top, black fishnet stockings, a long-sleeved white longjohn top, red lace bra set, a camouflage mini-skirt made out of a pair of sawed-off army pants and a pale blue and white-striped button-up shirt cut to fit a little boy.

She hmphed softly to herself and tried not to smile shyly as the last tears slid down her face.

"And you are so not wearing those bright red draws under that there short skirt to go rough-house with your little violent gang of Artboyz all day!" he growled.

"I didn't pick it out!"
"Fine! But you're putting bike shorts under that skirt!"Kahn yelled.

"What makes you think I'd lose and to be all bottoms up with'em anyway?" Anukai muttered, insulted.

"Up or down, I said No! The little-And as for the bra- luckily…there's another option." he said, flitting between emotionalized outbursts the way men flipped through channels with a remote, no residue from the previous one ever left behind.

Anukai smiled up at Kahn like little baby Jesus and held out her hand as Kahn dug into his pocket and gingerly tossed her a royal blue lace balconette bra she'd been wistfully designing in her head in physics class for the last two months, to the obvious dismay of Dr. Sanjivamurthy whenever she called on her.

"There's your little breastplate," Kahn muttered as she blush-grinned so big that her face looked like it was about to burst stroking the fragile lace the way most people stroked babies.

"You want the draws, or you want to wear the red bulls-eye ones I'm going to kick his little you know what over-"

"Gimmie-" she muttered, not even looking up. Kahn threw the matching boyshorts on her head and turned to walk out the window of the room.

"Still wear the bike shorts-Get your things from yer home- all of them this time-and be in study hall. On Time-" he called over his shoulder. "I'll see you in Ms. Harvey's class- On time."

"On Time," she mimicked then shuffled out of bed, into the shower, and off to the Cleveland Museum of Art.

## chapter thirty six

When Anais looked up, it was after one o'clock. She looked over at bear, whose entire production team was drenched with sweat after a job well-done.

"How many scenes did we shoot today?"she asked him professionally. Bear scribbled a number and passed it to her, too exhausted to even speak.

"333? Not bad, folks. Not bad at all. Good job! We're caught up to schedule. Let's call it a day for you dolls." A bell was rung  and a cheer went up through the crowd.

"Same time tomorrow." She sang out and tossed her beret up in the air, signaling she was no longer the director. The dolls filed off the set in an orderly manner to their various cubbyholes. Her stomach groaned with hunger as bear sleepily reminded her of  the actors needed for tomorrow's scenes scattered across the house on vacation. All had been called and were making their way to the TV room to be picked up.

She skipped down the stairs happily, music she had tuned out while shooting still softly rocking the house. She ran through the dining room, running back to grab the mug of cereal she'd completely forgotten about,. It was empty thanks to now fat tigers  sprawled around it with scruffs full of sugar smacks and bellies full of milk.  "No wonder I'm so hungry," she muttered and sped back to the kitchen through the TV room, stopping to kiss her trying-to-sleep Daddy on the cheek and step over her obviously bored brother sprawled all over the place.

She grabbed a Mango, went back into the TV room and plopped down on the floor in front of her dad, far enough from Fluke not to be bothered by him.

As soon as her teeth sank into the mango she remembered that they were going to a wedding and she squealed with her mouth full of fruit.

Her brother's eyes narrowed like he absolutely hated her joy. He looked at her with the spite only an older brother could call love. He went back to the martial arts movie playing with the sound off, the tracks her father had spinning re-scoring the movie.

"Uh Huh… you forgot, about the wedding, didn't you? Up there playing architect again, huh?' her groggy father murmured from the confines of the best couch in the world to fall asleep on, eyes shielded from the light by his hand like he always did when he slept. Anais nodded happily.  She'd given up explaining she didn't want to be an architect and instead just asked for dolls, cameras and houses every chance she got, figuring he'd get it eventually.

"Well, long as  you act right the rest of the day you can go. Take all your dolls upstairs too."

"Okay," Anais grunted around another mouthful of fruit and began collecting the rag-tag pile of dolls that had amassed in the den with one hand, sucking what  remained of the mango with the other. Fluke thought she didn't notice him perk up with interest when their father said 'long as' but she did.

Fluke looked around as if she'd just said I love you until his eyes settled on an ugly doll he called gummy because it smiled at him all the time. He grabbed it and pulled it into his lap, stroking it the way a lonely old lady would a cat. Anais threw the seed of the mango so that it sailed only inches over his head in warning  into the garbage can directly behind him.

Fluke looked up and smiled sweetly, his eyes narrowed.

*"If you get me in trouble, Imma kill you"* she hissed at him in the spirit. She nodded soundlessly at their dad, threw her head back and laughed maniacally.

On the TV screen behind them, Bruce Lee faced off with his nemesis on mute, dubbed over English replaced by the bass that throbbed in the house.

"Ha-ha," her brother laughed without moving his lips, the evil smile breaking out again. "Your threats are of no match for me," he yelled out with the movie he'd seen a thousand Saturdays, his face contorted just like the evil mastermind plastered across the screen. Their father took his hand off his face and looked at Fluke like he had lost his mind. He popped him in the back of the head with his knee. "Sorry, Flip," Fluke chuckled sheepishly. "Got caught up in-"

"Fluke… leave her alone…nah… you know what? I'm not telling you any more. Almost five years younger than you and already almost as big as you... and crazy like her moms-you'll learn." their Dad shuffled on the couch and yawned, almost instantly sleep.

All Fluke heard was he was not being told to leave his little sister alone anymore. He started stroking the stiffly smiling doll harder. Anais ignored him. *"Tell me Anaiiiiis, what's her name again~?"* Fluke sang out telepathically.

"My name is Calliope, you sociopath! now put me down! " the doll yelled out nervously, surprising him so much that he missed a beat. He looked down as the doll's face morphed from smile to scowl.

Fluke's spirit jumped out of him and glared at Anais, who acted as if nothing was happening at all. The shell of her brother sat there without his spite for a moment, eyes still narrowed.

*"If you get me in trouble, Imma kill you,"* she said in the spirit again. *"God, if he gets me in trouble I get to kill him-"*

Fluke's spirit started doing a sick waltz around with the doll's soul in front of her.

 Anais trembled. "Daddy," she called out softly, "Can I have a time-out?"

"…A time-out?" Her father asked incredulously without taking his hand off his face. The spirit of Fluke stopped short at the sound of his voice.

"A time-out. Cuz Fluke KNOWS I want to go to the wedding tonight, but he's going to get me in trouble so I can't go. But if you give me a time-out, then that's my punishment ahead of time, and I still get to go," she said breathlessly.

"Now see, that's from her hanging around all those white kids," Fluke grumbled conspiratorially and elbowed his father's knee, who opted to try to ignore his crazy children.

Fluke's spirit began to hum softly, *"du-du...du-dudu… du-du,"* mocking Anais,  unaware that the gift he was torturing her with had come directly from his pops, who saw every move the insane boy made in the spirit.  He tried not to laugh in his sleep as Fluke hummed, dancing with Calliope's soul to his sister's favorite Rick James song that had kicked back on like it was trying to help him ruin it for her.

"Daddy, can I PLEASE have a time-out!" she squealed, mad at herself because she knew the squeak let Fluke know he was getting to her.

"But you haven't done anything yet, Anais…" her father mumbled sleepily and rolled over.

"Whoah-oh-oh-oh-oh-ohoh-baby-yeah!" Fluke's spirit  sang out. The doll's face twisted in outright terror as Fluke began thrusting the butt of the doll roughly against his own in time to the music, the lyrics stuck in his head thanks to his kid sister's love of the song.

"Now sang it sugah-du-du..sang it girl-.du-du-du…du-du-"

*"Daddy,"* Lil Anais whispered tremulously in the spirit.
"..A Time-out? A Time-out- People are crazy!" he grumbled.
"Yeah,  have a time out. Whatever. Yeah-"

Instantly, Anais leapt up and clotheslined Fluke's spirit back into his body then pimp-slapped  Fluke so hard with her right hand that she knocked the sleep out of his eyes.

He screamed as Calliope went in the air,  gummy grin back on her face as she landed in the arms of  her momma. Anais popped Fluke in the head with her  doll hard enough to almost crack the plastic.

"Anais!Go to-!" Her father screamed as Anais squeaked "Time-out!" and ran out the room before being put on punishment. Her father tried not to laugh.

"Did you see what she did!?" Fluke roared, outraged.
"I told you," their father chuckled. "And your punishment-"
"Me?!" Fluke fussed.

"Yeah, you! You ARE going tonight, too. And you're going to carry records AND hold the door for your little sister that you love so much."

"Which door?!" Fluke yelped as if he'd been slapped again.

"All of them. And when she starts hopping around like a nut on the floor, if nobody else goes out there and dances with her, YOU are going to, or I will stop the music, come down and beat your yellow bowlegged ass." Fluke's mouth dropped open, but his father cut him off. "Every Song. Until She is TIRED." It was the ultimate betrayal.

Anais ran back into the room to pick up the other dolls she had left behind. Her hand-print  stood out in bright red on her brother's butter colored face. Fluke scowled at her as it registered to her  how hard she had hit him.

"Go to bed, Anais!" her father yelled, startling her as she looked at Fluke in awe- "Don't look at me, you did that!" he laughed. "Now go!…time-out."  Anais blushed, scooped up the last of her toys and ran out of the room.

"And smile!" Fluke's father seethed after she left.  "For every photo I get back with you not smiling, I am going to- you know what."

Fluke plastered on the biggest shit-eating grin he could muster. "Good," his father muttered. "And don't squeeze her hand either. Because however angrily she learns to play with you, her handsome, posed to be protective older brother, is exactly how violently she is going to end up playing with everyone else. Now go get my equipment loaded up so I can get some frickin' sleep."

**chapter thirty seven**

One was waiting for her on the loveseat built into the stairs. Arms full of toys, she started to defend her actions. God beamed love at her with no conditions until she stopped, mollified and mortified.

"I'm sorry." she whispered so softly that only he could hear it, climbed up and leaned against his chest. He didn't even have to say anything. She just knew. But she still didn't understand.

"I know I don't have to fight, you fight for me-and you fight better than me-but I'm really good at it, and it-it keeps coming out- and he- he makes it come out on purpose- If it's not supposed to be in there, why is it? I don't want to hurt him, but HE- he wants to hurt me- and… if it's bad to fight and I'm good-you say I'm good- then why do I know how to do it?"

God whispered an answer to a question she was too young to ask. The little girl burrowed her head into him even more as hot tears ran down her face in confusion. She looked up at him, unable to look anywhere but at the hairs of the thick silver and black eyebrows that waved at her one at a time.

"No. That's not it- you Are good! You are so good- Just because, too. Didn't hafta do anything to be good. And I love. You and your crazy big brother-" God continued softly. "All my kids are warriors. But you have to learn when, how, and what to fight or you'll wipe out your own side in the war without even realizing it…It's like taking your own men when you and your daddy play chess."

She furrowed her brow trying to get a picture to make sense of his words.

"But you can't take your own men in chess unless you go to the other side-oh!" she whistled as she got it.

"I'm sorry," she said again. "All the way now," she mumbled.

"I know,"God nodded.

Anais hopped down and scampered up the rest of the stairs towards her room.

**chapter thirty eight**

Fluke slumped out of the living room towards the side door lugging records and amps. He stopped short at the bathroom on the way back as  his hand crept up to his cheek. God leaned on the desk in the hallway, smirking. "Wanna see it?"

Fluke tried to act nonchalant. "Nah-"
'Good cause…" God whistled.
"What?!" Fluke yelped and ran into the bathroom. The little red hand-print  gleamed angrily on his face as he got mad all over again. Demons in the tiles responded to his dark shift  and started to seep into the bathroom.

"You betta not, Cain," God chuckled.
Fluke growled, "but look how-"
"Whose fault is that?" God laughed.
"I ain't hit her! Is this gonna fade before-" Fluke fussed.
"You worried 'bout yo pretty, boy?" God laughed. "And yeah, you ain't hit her today- but you taught her how to hit. Didn't you?"

"I ain't taught her," Fluke demurred, "nothin…"
"She clotheslined you-"
"That may be the case-" Fluke said smoothly. "Only God knows where she picked up such shenanigans-"he grinned innocently.

"Yeah! I do! From you, Fluke!" God laughed.
"I can't be held accountable for such uncivilized behavior-"

"You pulled her arm out, pushed yer mean lil hand against it to make her make it stiff and actually-" God muttered.

"That's all conjecture-"
"That's not conjecture, Fluke-"

"That's not the meaning of that word?" Fluke murmured innocently.

God made the mark redder.
"OK, OK, ok- I do seem to recall what could be… construed …as a clothesline tutorial…in court! But am I in court?" Fluke asked defensively.

"You sorry?" God asked.
"Yeah, sorry she hit me!" Fluke laughed.

God left him in the bathroom. "Hey! God! Come on! It- It's a start!" he called out.

**chapter thirty nine**

The child's guardian angel paced back and forth in a room filled with a Holier spirit he couldn't see. He was pensive, wondering what could be done on his side to temper the temper of the little "I am" who'd decided to be called "is" before she got there.

One watched the guardian pace back and forth like a nervous father, bemused by how attached the spirit had become to the girl. An idea popped into the guardian's head just as Anais got to the top of the stairs. Arms that had been loaded up with dolls gave way out in the hall.

"That's it," Anais muttered as she looked down at the pile. "We're close enough, you guys can walk home," she said curtly and walked off as one by one, the motley crew of dolls hopped up and ambled behind her like baby geese. She walked right through her guardian as she crossed the threshold, then spun around in glorified shock and grabbed where his leg would have been if he was human, happily holding onto thin air.

"I know you're here," she whispered, her voice muffled by spiritual things she could feel but not really see.

Her guardian beamed down at her like she was just as much his as she belonged to the father she had actually come through. He struggled to kneel down to greet her at eye-level as she vice-gripped a thigh even he hadn't felt prior to her focusing on it.

"Is Fluke bleeding?" he whispered.
"No, he's just light-skinned so it's red where I-" she muttered.

"Wait- were you there?" she asked precociously, "Did you see what he did?!"

"No. You were with your daddy, I don't need to be there when he's there, remember? But it echoed through the whole house-" the guardian confided.

Anais nodded and let go of the Angel's leg. "Fluke never stops. All the time- he just waits for a window!" she fussed.

"I know, but you picked each other to be siblings, so you knew what you were getting into."
"I know," Anais muttered, "but he's not doing it right!"
"Do you Want to kill him someday?" the Angel asked.

"Does he want to kill me?" she shot back hotly. "No, I don't want to kill him," she muttered aloud, "But I will if he won't leave me alone-"

The Angel interrupted her, "I want to introduce you to some friends of mine, Okay?"  Anais nodded shyly, embarrassed that he wanted her to meet anybody of his at all after what had happened the last time.

"WAIT, " he muttered, memory triggered by the guilty look on her face. "ProMISE me. ALOUD." he ordered.

She looked at him as darkly as she could in a room flooded with light. "I promise I won't hurt nobody." she whinnied defensively.

Soon as she said it, the room shifted in the reflection of it that beamed out of his glowing eyes.

**chapter forty**

The more twelfth-grade Gabryl stomped down the street to the bus-stop the more frenzied his thoughts became.

Images of things that didn't make sense blurred around him as he attempted to force each thought suctioned to his head out of his body through the force of his feet.

He'd been haunted by visions of his death ever since the attack on him as a child,  the farthest back his brain went. But he'd gotten through that, had carved an angry, caged existence around a few minutes of life on the other side of death that he'd never been able to explain or express to anyone after the fact. On an intellectual level it didn't matter to him, really. He'd already died a long time ago, no matter how many people told him he was crazy for thinking like that. And to him, the rot of the world smelled the same as it did when he'd first said fuck it.

But lately, it was different. This wasn't about a little boy. He was a man almost, not a kid with a bloody chest trying to learn how to want to live.  This time the death coming slammed into him like a schoolyard brawl, hitting his senses like shrapnel ahead of time. It popped in his ears like bullets on the blocks he'd already cursed God for having been born on.

He saw nothing around him but cracked concrete, cockroaches scurrying past in broad daylight and the fast-paced step of overpriced ugly tennis shoes classmates killed for.  He didn't see the demons storming down the street as clouds of flies behind him, hiding in the morning shadows of every other person in pain he'd silently slammed through trying to get to where he was going.

They gathered steam from the darkness that shot out of Gabryl's eyes in his outright refusal to process what he'd carried around for so long that he could not see.

Flies crushed  towards him like hornets, hungry for dead flesh that didn't realize it had stood up and walked, no longer letting itself be food for things that wanted no light alive in the world.

None of the beasts on his tail allowed themselves to ponder the special interest of below in this particular specimen. Whatever it was about him played out above their pay grade. It was just another day on the "Job."

He'd bow down to the violent thoughts sent after his scent like rabid dogs to bring him in, or they'd corrupt somebody to gun him down in the street the way they tended to in neighborhoods like this. He'd obey-the way they'd all learned to obey-or not, but either way this day would be his last.

A tsunami of bad thoughts slapped him around with each breath. It was so heavy in his head that his chin was bruised from physically burrowing into his chest.  He crashed into the two of them and ended up splayed out on the ground, never seeing them coming.

The cloud of flies following him exploded.

Gabryl looked up in shock at the raspy voice of a woman  as she reached down and yanked his bruised soul back up to the surface.

"Nice-boots, Kin." The woman murmured, playfully running her syllables together as she untangled her steel toed boots from his.

**chapter forty one**

Anais looked over her shoulder as three grown black women suddenly showed up behind her, all near the same strange shade of chocolate she was. Even seated they were tall. Taller than tall.

There was one who sat like the girls in the kung fu movies with her calves tucked under her atop a green silk pillow. A feathered Farrah Fawcett  hairdo fluttered down over her shoulders to the center of her back, just like the mother of Anais. She had on ripped-up, paint-splattered jeans, a white tank-top, and had karate shoes tucked in her back pocket. The woman smiled with her eyes like she was about an inch from crazy, but on purpose.

The next one was sprawled like a boy across a plush, red winged chair in black latex slashed open so she could breathe, held together suggestively with chrome-plated quills and safety pins that matched the armless reflective aviators that balanced gingerly on her nose.  Her hair shot out in a cottony-white halo a good twenty-four inches across. She never smiled and you could tell at first sight.

But it was the third one that levitated upside down in the air between the two of them that made Anais turn all the way around. The little girl stared into the upside down face in front of hers and smiled like never before.

The woman blush-grinned back and flipped right side up. The satiny scarf  tied around thick ringlets came undone and her hair undulated out.

She had on draw-stringed pants and a tube top that matched the same shade of electric blue that she had stroked across the lid of only one eye. Words in a language Anais didn't understand cascaded up her arms in darker and lighter shades of blue all the way over the edge of her jaw line.

The blue lady smiled and curtsied to the little girl the way Anais curtsied to everyone she actually liked, then nestled down onto a pillow that was covered in the same silk shantung her pants had been cut from. She pulled out a pair of green glasses splattered with red and blue that had been hidden in her top to get a better look at the child. The multicolored assortment of jeweled bracelets on her forearms screamed out for attention just as much  as everything else about the woman did.

The shiny black woman roughly threw a red shantung pillow from her chair on the ground and sprawled on it like a boy.

"Anais, I'd like you to meet Alekto, Babylon and Motoko," her Guardian Angel motioned towards them.

Motoko pushed her glasses up and beamed love to the little girl who was yet another one who could somehow see what she wasn't supposed to, the words on her flesh dancing happily because of it.  The crazy-eyed, paint splattered lady nodded insanely on purpose.

Anais looked back at her guardian shyly.

"POD- Propaganda. Offense. Defense." her Guardian murmured as he motioned to each one in accordance to their specialty, ruffling the kid's hair so it would unfurl.

"Fight School?!" Anais yelped excitedly and corkscrewed up in the air for joy.

"Yeah," Alekto yelped, wild-eyed.
"So you don't kill nobody." Motoko laughed.
"That doesn't really, really deserve it-" Babylon snarled almost happily.  Motoko swatted at Babylon, who laughed roughly, exposing the most beautiful, big teeth Anais had ever seen in her life.

She cocked her head to the side for a better look."Can I have her teeth?" she asked.

"You'll have to fight me for them," Babs growled.

"Yeah… It's time you really learned how to dance." Motoko whispered hoarsely, a bizarre smile splayed across her face.

## chapter forty two

Gabryl looked up at the chick still standing after all 180 pounds of him had slammed into her like a mac truck.

Above the consciously violated boots that ensconced her feet sat thick heather-flecked army socks pulled over fishnets, all of which was usually hidden from the world by the patchwork silk ball-gown skirt that she wore in outright visual contrast to the skintight de-constructed blazer that pretended to be trying to cover her upper half. Above the deep v of it, all but the nipples of pert breasts were rammed up and out into daylight by a black fishnet balconette bra like cicadas resting atop tree limbs. Below it, even on a day as oddly chilly as this one, the expanse of her browned hips and her belly button pulsed with such heat that he swore he saw a bead of sweat sliding down it and soaking into the long skirt he had inadvertently been looking up.

"A little discretion, Kin… please~" purred the guy who had been walking alongside her in the most gentlemanly way. He roughly snapped his fingers a few times to break Gabryl out of his daze.  Gabryl's head whipped around to take in the dude, face flushed as the guy grabbed and easily pulled him back up onto his feet. "She's asked me to kill for less on her behalf," the man said conspiratorially.

Embarrassed, Gabryl focused on dusting himself off. *"Clubheads,"* he thought to himself. *"Have to be"* "

"I'm...I'm really sorry, I-" Gabryl stumbled around inside of himself looking for words. The effort made his face hurt, like he hadn't spoken for five years.

"...wasn't paying attention to things. We know," the craggly-voiced woman purred.  "No worries. I know you meant no harm. I can tell everything I need to know about you by your shoes."she said softly.

Gabryl looked in her eyes. Her irises had as many colors bouncing around in them as  her gear. He was still a bit confused as what she said hit him. He looked at her feet, then his, and then over towards those of her gentleman friend. All three had on battle-scarred combat boots in the middle of the rough yet cosmopolitan city.

The flies began to plot their ways back towards him in full spiritual sight of the couple. The woman slowly raised a brow at her associate as he almost imperceptibly tightened his jaw. He started to slowly pace around the woman and the teenaged boy in the middle of morning rush hour.  With each step the guy took, territory was taken back.

Ulterior Angels popped into view one at a time along either edge of the sidewalk, a gauntlet of angelic spirits the kid had not even known he had walked straight through. They stood at stone-faced attention as the underground corporeal made the silent force of his spiritual rank known behind an oblivious Gabryl. With each Angel's appearance, another cluster of flies snapped,crackled and popped into view as demons. Their charred bodies fell as the Ulterior gauntlet slashed into action. The gentleman smiled with soft satisfaction as ancient prose welled up to the surface of his spirit and seeped out in song.

"There is more of me with you than  them coming for you; you have with you the only one you need; if God be for you-who on Earth can be against you?"

His black cashmere pants were thinly pinstriped with the same chaotic colors that danced across the vision that was her. He was always cold for her hot, so the perfectly cut matching blazer that he wore had the knubbiest navy turtleneck sweater shoved underneath it, which made him look even broader across the shoulders than he already was. The multi-flecked Kangol he wore was tilted to the side, and strange shocks of locked hair stuck out where it hadn't been shorn and cut into with glyphs. His brows were angular slashes across his face, with features that could be beautiful yet flare up into terrifying rage in an instant. He moved with such elegance and grace that nobody but her dared to tangle with him.

The woman cleared her throat. "I'm Cyda." "This," she said, motioning towards her partner, "Is my brother Krystian. We call him Astaire." The elegantly violent rogue  Astaire whirled around with a flourish and bowed gently. "Related? Yes, but by things beyond blood-" she murmured, running the words together once again because she was addicted to the vibration that rocked her when she did.

Astaire nodded "All clear" to the stern sister he called Cyd. She leaned into Gabryl's ear and began to speak words to him that made no sense to his head but buoyed his heart as Astaire paced the perimeter again just in case.

The sheer number of the felled minions made Astaire look again at the kid a Comptroller named Kahn had asked to be zone bountied for the day sans full explanation of what was up.

"Who" Kahn was... none of that mattered too much to Astaire. Some called him VayoKahn, others just Vayo, while others underground intimated that he was somehow connected to the origin of Others and Ones a long time ago.

What Astaire and Others like him did know is that this particular Comp had nothing to do with this territory beyond three-ins-and- outs in conjunction with the boy who'd grown up before their eyes with no other guardian angel synched to him, good or bad. But Kahn's words echoed in Astaire's head

"…Just in case they try to yank him. Again."

The metallic sound that Kahn's voice took had told Astaire things that even his elevated self would not have been able to explain if he had to. Luckily, the response was the same to his Cistern-in-the-flesh Cyd.  They both knew they'd defend this gangly kid as if fighting for their own right to life unrestrained in this world below they had swam through a watery hells together to get to.

Astaire also didn't know exactly whose Ulteriors those were in the kid's wake. He peered at them through the spirit as people passed by. You could usually tell. But as he took in the mounds of dead flies that had been blown by the wind up against garbage cans in heaps, he realized that it didn't matter. Whoever these Ulteriors belonged to, he was glad they were on the same side.

When Astaire looked back at Cyd, she was sliding the small slip of wildly printed acetate into one of the pockets of Gabryl's beat-up fatigues.

"Lil-Bruh …When it gets too real, and I have the sneaking suspicion it is about to …come here." Cyd whispered, patting the flyer in his pocket.  "But for now …take your wiry ass to school."she growled. Gabryl nodded.

"Cyd~" Astaire snapped softly, tilting his head as the ship they'd been ordered to make sure he got onto came in.

She smiled and pulled away from him, letting him look at her one more time. "Remember." shot out of her eyes like an order as she walked on.  It hit Gabryl's face like the protective kiss on the cheek from a big sister he never had until that moment.

Gabryl knew better than to say bye. He somehow knew they were already gone.

But the interaction with the ones who called themselves Cyd like Charisse and Astaire had been enough to pull his head a bit above water.

He was snapped out of his thoughts by the screeching tires of a city bus. The driver slammed on the horn and opened the doors at the same time.  When Gabryl saw who was driving, his almost atrophied facial muscles pulled into a rictus grin.

## chapter forty three

The red-boned young-blood JuanJon nodded a what-up as the lanky kid he used to baby-sit stomped onto the bus.

A former Marine, he was back stateside keeping the masses free-flowing after multiple sets out in the red sands of the Middle East.  He'd taught Gabryl how to fight without trying to kill folks as a kid and had once driven a tank over shit so tough that word had gotten back to the hood months before he did.

The bus was full of old church folks Gabryl usually avoided after they'd captured his moms from all she had been doing off in the cut a forever ago. The spiritual biddies went silent in prayers of protection over the boy as he pulled his wallet out and unfolded it.

Gabryl's jaw dropped upon seeing the corner of a crayon covered slip of paper that he had thought he'd lost years ago reappearing where he once had known he'd put it. His pained smile twisted up into something that was so grisly that wiry Driver JuanJon  yelled at him, pulling him  back out of his thoughts.

"Yo, Gabryl! What the hell, man?" Gabryl looked up, the odd smile still on his lips. "Man, go sit the Ef down! And wipe that crazy Fn grin off yo face! Ugh! I need to beat yo Fn-"

He waved Gabryl on to the bus without paying as a horde of people who'd appeared out of nowhere pushed forward recklessly.

"Jesus Christ! Yo! What the Ef does this look like?! Jesus Christ!" JuanJon roared, stunning the crowd.  The old ladies in the front of the bus gasped in horror at the almost profanity.

"Aight-Aight-" he muttered as he spread apologies across the saintly women he'd grown up seeing be evil as hell on many occasions before they'd gotten sanctified in old age. He shut the doors of the bus in front of the people outside who still wanted to get on and stood up.

"Full!" he barked so loud that all that had pushed onto the bus before he locked the door got silent in the stairwell  along with everyone else. The scowl on his face twitched at the respect shown for his authority.

"Look here, My name is Master Gunner Sergeant JuanJon Lucas Jenkins- I come from a little town they used to call New York Fn City!" he roared with all 165 pounds of his tightly wound body that had 237 kills to its credit out in the battlefield.

"And this here bus is MY Tank! You will do what I say! Or you will find another way to your destination! You will get off NOW! Any Takers?" he paused and looked around menacingly before he carried on.

"Good! Now we can have an easy ride to where you decided you need to go at this time in your everlasting life! OR-we can have it hard, like I had it out there fighting on behalf of your asses in the red desert for six years back to back! Your sanctified selves in particular," he growled at the old ladies from his block.

"So take those FN bags down off those FN seats and let FN people sit the Ef down! And Everybody shut the Ef up so we can get the Ef to where the Ef we all gots to FN go!"

One of the little kids inside of Gabryl that he had ignored for forever chuckled as all the mean old ladies now following the True God hmphed and pulled out fans with sepia-toned prints of Dr. Martin Luther King on one side, adverts for reconstructive surgery marketed to seniors on the other.

"They're probably praying for me with each breath, like it'd even matter," Gabryl muttered to himself. He opened the wallet still in his hands, pulled out the beat-up piece of paper and unfolded It. The image of him as a little boy with a Superman cape had returned, but this time, there were bullets coming towards him. He was surrounded by other figures in red capes just like his. The little girl who had been cheering him on in the drawing a lifetime ago was flying towards him in a cape of her own, looking over her shoulder at something off the page with a scared but angry frown drawn on her face.

Gabryl looked up in disbelief. Across the aisle, a younger version of himself sat sulking out the window. The light bouncing off the white of his little t-shirt and wetness on his face let the teenaged him know he'd been crying.

"Where is she?" the little boy cried out softly. "She's supposed to be here- she has to know it's today- where is she?" The little boy couldn't see the little girl right there with him, crying in confusion,  talking to him without him hearing.

"You're going to have to fight!" the little girl kept  screaming. Suddenly the little boy's shirt got soaked through with blood so red that big Gabryl inhaled incorrectly and exploded into a coughing fit, trying to shake the vision of it off.

Many of those who had pushed onto the bus directly behind him moved towards where he was seated, darkness and hate splayed across their cheeks as they turned away from him, completely blocking him  from anybody at the front of the bus. Whenever JuanJon tried to get a good look back the people shuffled unnaturally, as if trying to hide something. Old ladies up front broke into soft hymns of protection and salvation due to the sudden spirit of unease coating the bus.

"You really think she actually exists? Are you really that fucking crazy?" a soft sinister voice muttered next to him, loud enough for only him to hear as his neighbors slammed fists into his back, trying to help. Bewildered, Gabryl spun around and glared at the old man the chiding  had seemed to come from.

"What did you say?" Gabryl snarled at the harmless looking old man as he shoved the drawing back into his wallet and rammed it into the chest pocket of the tee he had on under Byblos's coat without even thinking about it.

"Do you know what time it is?" The old man repeated slowly, peering with curiosity at the one young enough to be his grandkid if he'd ever had kids. The old man wore weathered black cords, a sweater and shirt under an old car coat with silky, curly fur covering it that almost looked like human hair depending on the light.

Suddenly the old man growled.

 "It's time! Even if she did know what day it is, what can she do? I mean Look at you!" the gnarled old man in the human hair coat intimated darkly, pointing to the bloodied boy across the way to let Gabryl know they could both see him.

"Your little friend couldn't do anything then- you couldn't even tell her because you Knew you deserved it-and even If she could do Anything to help you now- You've already given up! It is all over your face! Even you know that you can't fight it!" the senior hissed.

The bus lurched to a stop as JuanJon slammed on the breaks to avoid hitting a Cadillac that had run a red light, throwing the whole bus into a fit. The sanctified Seventh Day Adventist women his moms had begun acting like started falling out under the power of the Holy Spirit as it hit the bus.

"Praise the Lord!" yelled two or three ladies at the same time as others in menopausal hot-flashes talked in tongues, fanning themselves at the same time.

"Devil, I rebuke you!" clusters of them screamed.
"Devil! YOU will take no one on this here bus Today!"
"He is not yours! He is dedicated! HE belongs to God!!"
"HIJO DE Dios-" Some old ladies screamed in Spanish.
Even a gaggle of little Chinese women in the middle of the bus started going off about Jesus in Cantonese and Mandarin.

"YOU know where you belong! You don't' Belong here! Somebody owns you! Even you know that Today is the day you're going to die!" the old man screeched in Gabryl's terrified face.

The back doors of the bus flew open and Gabryl leapt off of it out into traffic. Those that had crowded onto the bus after him tried to follow behind him but the angels of the old ladies started to beat down the beasts inside the bus on his behalf.

The frail old man who called himself the Advocate in certain circles nestled quietly into his still cold seat in satisfaction.

Ever the chameleon, he started to chime in with the shouts of deliverance exploding out of the old biddies in order to blend into the cacophony, albeit softly.

"Yo, Gabryl! Gabryl!" JuanJon yelled after the fatigues-clad kid as he cut in front of the bus, making Gabryl stop short in the middle of the street.

"WHAT!?!?" Gabryl roared back, his body pulsating with enough rage and fear to take out a city block if he had to. JuanJon had seen that look before, right before a member of his unit went crazy and did just that.  JuanJon locked eyes with Gabryl and saw the same thing that had been there as a kid who had survived things JuanJon knew not one adult with the constitution to.

A car that thought it was going to run right through the accident scene slammed on its breaks and stopped just inches from taking out Gabryl at the knees. The driver blared his horn in protest. Gabryl momentarily whipped his head towards the driver with such ferocity that the driver flinched and ripped his hands off the wheel.

*"It is going to be alright, man."* JuanJon whispered telepathically to him the way he used to do against the top of his head when the boy would crack and have to be pulled off of this or that neighborhood bully, covered in the bully's blood and his own tears. *"It's gone be Aight-"*

Gabryl looked up at JuanJon as if he'd been splashed with ice cold water, a memory transmitted between the two of them that slashed at the anger and fear plastered across him. He shook it off and started running again, not stopping until he got to the bottom of the steps leading to the outer grounds.

**chapter forty four**

By the time Anukai could see the corner, the bus was already barreling down the road. She broke into a run towards it, blasting through slow-moving kids working up the courage to cut school.

The driver saw her coming and narrowed his eyes, doing his best to slam the doors shut just to see what she'd do. Ten yards away she snorted defiantly and sped in the direction the bus was going to have to head anyway, giving the guy the finger as she flew past him. Her fishnet-encased legs stretched behind her in a blur, the sprint effortless, cockiness already splayed across her features in the long-range surveillance cams they both knew he had to behave on that were strung up at the intersection where the next stop was or temporarily be suspended like the last time he sped by her on purpose.

Even though she didn't smoke, by the time he had arrived at the light she could have already bummed a cigarette, took a puff and held it in just to blow it in his face, which she had done two years ago before pointing out to him mid-leer that she was just as underage as always on a crisp spring morning.

The driver snarled and slammed his foot on the gas in hot pursuit of his morning route arch-enemy. She was the reason he'd given up coffee and taken up smoking cigarettes to calm down at the end of any shift the little daemon was on his bus.

"Good Morning!" she chirped as he slowly pushed the doors halfway open to make her wedge her way in. She snarled and pointed to the camera capturing the pained performance she erupted into as all the color drained from his face. "Ow! Oh my God-OW! My Arm! My Arm! Why won't you open the door all the-"

He smiled weakly and mouthed "So Sorry!" for the camera as he let her on. She turned her head away from the camera and glowered at him then sauntered onto the bus.

"Malak-" the driver muttered under his breath.
"Yah moms, overgrown Latent!" Anukai barked back. "Want to hit on my underage ass some more to feel better about the perverted ass you've grown into? Fucking pedophile."

She settled into a seat right up front just to mess with him in his rearview mirror, as was  the dance everyday she didn't cut school. The other regulars on the commute rolled their eyes and slid right back into being lost in the vibrations of the wheels on the bus going round and round all the way to wherever they were always were headed at  this hour.

The ride got more cramped when they got to University Circle due to the hospitals, high schools and colleges densely clustered around the area.  Anukai got off the bus at the water.

Wade Lagoon shimmered under the unseasonably warm sun behind the Cleveland Museum of Art. She hopped down the steps to it and picked her way through families of geese and goldfish she had grown up alongside towards her other home like a big kid.

**chapter forty five**

Her combat boots thudded past the replica of the Thinker she'd been told not to touch so many times that her fingerprints had become a part of the piece.

The guards stood at attention, angry scowls in place. They were ready to play gatekeeper with one of the offs, their nickname for the wild bunch of kids who'd been running sock-footed through the galleries of the museum since they were toddlers.

"What up, profs-" Anukai grinned with a toss of her chin in a hood nod of respect. The two elder artists guarding her home of homes looked at each other then cocked their heads to the side at the same time. *"Who do you think you are" was*  incised into their stony features, refusing her unspoken request for entry.

"Aw-come on!!!!" she whined.
"No..." They said in unison. The old Columbian Santiago tried to keep the twinkle out of his eye as the wind whipped his pelvic bone length hair up in response to her pouting.

"I'm late for school!" she whimpered almost convincingly.

"You were Late for school an hour ago-" The old men said sarcastically at the same time. The one called Rubio due to the ruddy color that was only at the tip of his nose said it a bit slower than the other, letting her know which one would be the first to break.

"...Rubio!"she cried out.  He stiffened.

He'd known  the child for more than a decade. She thought she lived there and left pieces of herself behind every time so as to prove it to anyone crazy enough to challenge her on it.

Anukai twisted her face up into exactly the same sad scowl that had got him to cover for her at age three when he'd caught her drawing fish scales on the blond floors of the Assyrian gallery to match the skirt of the wall carving she used to always be found under when she'd gone missing.

"...At least she wasn't drawing on the artifact!" was how he'd explained his decision to do so to higher ups when the incriminating footage surfaced.

Santiago's hair kicked up again. His eyes flashed white for an instant to draw her back to him."Stop bullying him! Do you know how much damage they-"

"I promise to get them all this time!" she sang quickly.
"You always promise that, and then I have to explain why this and that has your sticky-" Rubio fussed gruffly then pouted in perfect imitation of her.

"But This time, I came Just to make sure I picked up ALL of-em, me- I mean-" her words tumbled out nervously. "I really mean it this time," she promised.

They both rolled their eyes and stepped  out of her way at the same time, giving her passage. "Go! But YOU don't live here!" they both barked after her.

"I know! I know!"she curtsied and ran into the museum  before plodding back and pecking both of them on their cheeks.

"…But they do!" she whispered gleefully and ran back into the vestibule.

Inside, she looked up at the ceiling of her favorite place and let its atmosphere soak into her again.

High off of it and happy, she let out a furious yowl.

Aspects of her scattered all over the Cleveland Museum of Art looked up towards the sky-lights. They did their best to wrap up whatever games they had afoot with the guardians protecting the art from them.

**chapter forty six**

Anukai looked down the armor court as a six year old
version of herself leapt off a war horse in full samurai regalia.

Her sword blazed towards a bony, knock-kneed guard as tall as
she had been still on the horse. A war cry roared out of him,
shield raised, ready to fight back.

The guardian and the little child encased in leathery armor
stopped mid-clash, bowing to one another before the little one
scampered towards Anukai, flinging off her costume on the
way. She looked up at her larger self and blushed, Tengu
warrior mask pushed up off her face.

"Give it back," Anukai muttered toughly, trying not to smile at
the memories that fought so hard to stay close to this place. Her
six year old self smiled and tossed the priceless mask up in the
air. It was caught effortlessly by the guardian who'd made his
way over to pat her on the head.

"You're Taller," the guard muttered sheepishly.
"I'm always Taller. We grow~ " she muttered back, trying not
to smile.

"African, Psyche,  Indian, Chinese, and Japan." he mumbled
nonchalantly, as if they were talking about summer peas."And
one keeps getting kicked out of the Holy Family Room for
messing with the gilt. She  sits with her cheek pressed up
against the glass, giving the evil eye to all who come in."
"Got it. Thanks."
"And hurry up and go to school!" he barked.

Anukai raced through the galleries gathering aspects of herself like a mother goose.  Between orders of "put it back" museum guards wrangling wild kids in every nook and cranny of the place yelled out for her to go to class.

As Anukai made her way through the Asian galleries to the one who was always one of the last to be pulled away, a hush fell over the crowd of herself.

They all looked around the saffron stained corner that led to India at the little girl with one thumb in her mouth and the other hand looped around the fingers of a brown man stained blue with indigo. His silky hair fell away from him in waves and his shoulders were drenched in garlands of flowers. Another brown guy sat cross-legged on the floor. He was swaddled in cascades of orange fabric and his hair was twisted up into tiny corkscrew locks that bloomed  in a stubby ponytail at the top of his head.

"But why a bodhisattva, of all things, IDhar? And why is it so sad, INha?" The little one said around her thumb, peering into the face of a  strangely melancholy sculpture.

"For the same reason we all are," the blue one she called INha began.  The one on the floor smiled softly and cleared his throat, causing the blue man and child to see Anukai peeking around the corner.

"I'll tell you later," IDhar whispered and pulled the little one into his arms for a quick hug. INha bent down and pressed a gentle kiss to the top of her head, and they both pushed her towards the crew of Anukai as a tiny lotus bloomed atop the child like a crown.

All parties sighed dreamily over the idea of INha's lips on their face and scampered up out of the basement of the museum on a cloud.

They picked up the toddler scowling at gold-crusted paintings of little baby Jesus and his mama through the glass doors to the gallery at  the last moment to avoid as much fighting as possible. As Anukai turned away, di Lorenzo's baby Jesus stuck out its tongue  and laughed before putting its finger innocently back in its mouth.

"...Leave it," Anukai muttered before the offended little kid in her could throw a fit, "it's just a painting of a fat baby-I don't know why you keep letting him get you-"

As they burst through the same doors they'd come in as one once Anukai was lost within her thoughts.  She turned towards school, trying to ignore the rumbling in her stomach kicked up by the fresh air.

"Stop!-" Rubio and Santiago yelled in unison from behind her. "I want a head-count!" Rubio roared from the museum portico. "Already on it," Santiago chuckled.

 Anukai turned around with a playful dark look on her face. "What makes you think I left anybody behind?" she shouted  as the younger aspects of herself spun back out of  her, arms folded over every chest as Santiago assigned them each numbers with a gentle shove to the forehead.

"Twelve!" Rubio shouted. "I knew it! I knew it-which one of the little hooligans is missing?"
"HOOLIGANS~?! I've not broken a thing in there since I was like-seven!" Anukai fussed hotly.

Santiago scratched his chin as he inspected the usual suspects to see if any of them would dime out the missing link.

None of them budged. He leaned down so that he was eye to eye with the one who always had her thumb in her mouth. She narrowed her eyes at him.

"It's the twisted lil Blood god priestess, again" Rubio muttered.

"Hey! I didn't say!" The thumb-sucking kid fussed.

"You know where she is-" chuckled Santiago.
"Already on it," Rubio growled and did his best to keep a straight-face.

"Mateo/Tigris-over." he barked into his static filled walkie-talkie. "ETA on the MIA Blood God-" Rubio's eyes whited out as more static erupted in reply.

"He'll have her on her bloody little way," Santiago laughed.
"You know one of them is probably already sacrificed-" Rubio  smirked.

"Whatever!" Anukai blushed hotly as aspects of her ran off to play with geese and goldfish while they waited for the one who always found a way to be left behind.

## chapter forty seven

Ears lit, Tigris paced back and forth in front of the painting of Cupid and Psyche as children happily tucked into bed with one another. Every sort of sacred love beamed out into the space.

That day's mother and child class was camped out in one corner of the gallery. In another, inner-city kindergarten kids lulled into submission by paint and the license to be barefoot in the museum were sprawled out on polished floors.

Tigris knew where the little one nicknamed the Blood God was, and did everything he could to ignore the current of energy that was begging him to come and intervene in what his other half and her danced through every time they found one another on the museum grounds.

But today Tigris was being stubborn. He was not going to move from his location. The other one was going to have to get out of it himself.

He paced in front of the large painting so much so that some kids drew him in their pictures. He slammed his hand into the walkie-talkie purring with static inside of his pocket, pulled it out and hissed.

"Dude! I know you heard them! Bring her in, she has to go to-"

More static.

"Come on, man! You're-"

## chapter forty eight

The one called Mateo was sprawled on a stone slab altar at the center of the Pre-Columbian galleries in the basement of the Cleveland Museum of Art.

When he blinked he could see lit torches around him one moment, glistening golden artifacts the next, but for the life of him he couldn't move his body beyond his eyeballs in their sockets. Off to his left side, a brightly colored bird danced erratically, flapping wings full of brilliant red, blue and green feathers. Only it was too big to be a bird, and hopped around like a little kid having a sugar fit.  Mateo moaned as his line of sight slid towards his toes and he saw his chest was already wet with blood. The static surrounding him stopped.

"Wait a minute!" he screeched. "Why am I bleeding-did you do it already?!"

The colorful bird carrying on with its back to him stopped dancing and turned around. A huge beak obscured most of the child's face, but not enough to hide La Magra's identity. She smiled and slowly shook  her head no as she lifted up a golden chalice and took a long dreg from it.

"Then why the-Why-why am I covered in blood already?! Whose blood is this?!" Mateo roared.

The little girl pushed her mask up in shock. "His!" she fussed indignantly and pointed to the head of the bird she'd skinned out in a jungle only the two of them saw spread out below the stepped pyramid they were atop.

"You covered me in bird blood?! Let me up! Let me-why

can't I move my arms?! Wait-What are you drinking?!" Mateo yelled, laughing at the same time as she flashed him how she imagined one would have to scalp a big bird for its coat of feathers. He was suddenly aware that he was able to lift his head again.

"No! I'm not done yet!" the little girl howled and pouted, slamming his head back down on the stone before smiling crazily into his eyes. "But… Almost," she said sweetly and took another long drink.

"And this is Mole sauce," she purred, raising the holy grail in the air above her head happily as if she were getting a refill of ambrosia from the gods. The crackle of static started again as she shoved cacao leaves in his mouth with her free hand to continue alleviating the pain.

"Well hurry up, you hear them calling me to bring you in-" he muttered as he chewed.

"..I'm on the lam," she giggled.
"I know, you're always on the lam-across space and time-now finish -I mean me-you know what I-" Mateo tried to growl seriously. "And don't be sloppy! Bird blood? Ugh! Hurry up-"
"Okay, okay-"

La Magra sat the chalice down and danced around the altar one more time, arms out as if she were sailing through the air like the bird on her back once did.  She stopped and pulled out a ruby-encrusted gold dagger from beneath the feathers that glinted in the torch-light. She raised it up as both of them sucked air through their teeth.

"*Çan nomaccah in nix in noyollo inic ni nouatzaz. anoço inic ninocueponaltiz~* It is only by my hand, by my face, my heart, my spirit that either I will wither, or I will bloom, I will become as green land, as tilled earth I will germinate, I will sprout. ~" she squealed.

Mateo called on all kinds of Holies across three languages as the blade slammed down into his chest. The child roughly cut with her right hand then quickly plunged her left into him and pulled out his heart of Darkness, holding it up to the sky with a triumphant roar. The Citizens of the kingdom below she'd forgotten to flesh out cheered.

La Magra turned the heart upside down over her head and baptized herself in the red-black blood like the well-versed Olmec priest she knew she once was. She held his pulsing heart in her hands and danced around with it, laughing as all the black matter that had infected it rose to its surface and trickled down her tiny forearms.

"I did it! I did it!" she squealed, leaping in the air and landing so hard that her earrings clanged together like bells.

Mateo's head lolled over towards her. He watched all that had done so much damage to his heart evaporating quickly and fading back into a gallery in the basement of the Museum as the kid played in his chest.

"Is it clean yet?" Mateo whispered from his metaphysically trussed position.

Suddenly La Magra became very clinical about the whole thing, hopping up alongside him on the altar and peering into his open chest cavity past where his heart would normally be.

"Well…this is clean," she said tersely as she placed his heart atop his belly, "But whatever is in there is just going to get it dirty all over again if we don't clean it out."

Mateo nodded.

"What is it, anyway?" La Magra asked like a curious child instead of an all-knowing priest of the Blood God.

Mateo struggled for the most honest thing to say about something even he didn't fully understand. "...Memories." he whispered.

"Ugh. Get rid of them then, because I am not going to be around all the time to do this for you. Stop remembering, OK?" La Magra ordered stoically.

Mateo nodded as she dug into his chest and started scooping out the residual dark matter like a child happily playing in the mud. When she had gotten most of it out, she lifted her chalice, closed her eyes as she blessed it and turned it upside down over his sternum. Icy salt water gushed out, flooding the hole where his heart kept trying not to be.  She pulled more cacao leaves from a pouch underneath her wings and gingerly lined the inner cavity before rinsing the cleansed heart off and placing it in the nest she'd made.

By the time she was done, Mateo was stitched up and leading the bloody little child in the direction of her waiting party.

**chapter forty nine**

Gabryl froze against the wall along the stairs, looking up at his graffiti-scarred, soon to be alma-mater for what felt like an eternity. He scowled as his hatred for the place re-asserted itself then  forced himself to head in to his inner city high school campus.

He held the trembling hand of his inner child. The twin brother of his inner kid furiously untied his boots, tears flooding out of him as violent, ignorant, uneducated kids trapped in the thickening bodies of useless adults pushed past.

Gabryl hissed at himself, pulled his free hand out of his pocket and knocked the wet-faced kid away from his feet, then bent down to re-lace them.

He didn't notice the ink from the flyer smearing his hand due to fear and rage burning in his stomach. He angrily wiped at his own eyes and his oddly sweating forehead, since he was deathly cold. The dull ache in his chest made it all worse.

"Pussy," a thug barked as he shoved past Gabryl hunched over like he could smell the tears flowing down his face.

"Don't go in there today." his inner child whispered.
"…leave me Alone." Gabryl grumbled.

"No! Don't make me go!" wailed his inner kid's twin as he slammed the full weight of  his spiritual body into Gabryl's legs  as Gabryl stood back up, waving the twin visions of him as a kid off.

"Stop!" he hissed and shoved the two spirit boys away so hard that they were flung into the other side of the outer stairwell.

"We're not going through it again!" they screamed in unison, knocked into him and tore off down the street.

Gabryl bumped against a burly dude by mistake whose eyes flickered in recognition. He'd been in the banquet at Embryan the night before.

"Yo! Why you touch me, Faggot?" DUNO snarled in Gabryl's face, always waiting for an opportunity to prove he wasn't no bitch. He shoved Gabryl so violently that his head smacked the brick wall behind him and made him bite down roughly on the inside of his jaw. Bewildered, Gabryl tasted blood in his mouth, but felt no pain.

DUNO's boys cackled like the clutch of thuggish DLs they were, which made something in Gabryl chuckle at the wrong time. DUNO good's eyes went black. "You laughing at me, you little bitch?"

Unconsciously, Gabryl swallowed the blood pooling in his mouth and suddenly his eyes went all black too, then to full-on all white that only DUNO could see.

"Well....I wasn't," Gabryl whispered hoarsely, and spat a stream of blood on the ground not even a centimeter from DUNO's pristine white, high-jacked sneakers, "But-" Gabryl peered into DUNO's face and it dawned on him where he'd seen him. Rage blipped quietly up to the surface of Gabryl almost imperceptibly.

DUNO's left eye flinched and he knew that Gabryl saw it.

He swiftly pulled out a gun and stepped so close to Gabryl that no one passing by could see him press the barrel to his chest.

Gabryl absently looked past the thug and down the block at his inner kids. They had turned around, coated in bewilderment he could see from a quarter-mile away.

*"But It didn't happen outside,"* the kids said in unison, frozen in confusion.

"What you gone do now, bitch?! Laugh now! What you gone do?!" DUNO snarled as spittle from his lips scattered across Gabryl's face.

Gabryl closed his eyes calmly then opened them again. They flickered back and forth between white and black like a TV on the wrong channel. Something Latent in Gabryl laughed as it rose all the way up, awake, fully aware and at the wheel for the first time in forever.

"Iono…Die?" Gabryl asked lightly, "Then again, seeing as though we've already been down this road before…and I'm Here…all over again-" he smirked as he took in the ghat. "… looks like the same gun too," he chuckled darkly, "you never know-"

"Yo! DUNO! Put that shit up!" His younger brother NONO barked, not wanting to have to explain the shit to their moms. "That weird dude ain't even worth it," called out another. "Yo! Five-OH!" hissed the appropriately named Lookout.

About 10 yards back, a cluster of cops assigned to the school made their way towards the thugs like dogs shepherding the programmed to be criminals into their prison of a  school before they even got all the way on the scene.

They'd been dealing with DUNO and his boys for the six years they'd been stuck there so far.  DUNO-also known as Duane Norris when his moms had to pick his often suspended ass up-had been stuck in tenth grade for three years.

DUNO leaned close enough to deliver a kiss of death to Gabryl and whispered "This ain't done-"

The awakened Aware in the center of Gabryl laughed loud enough to be heard by the thug. It looked down at the gun and wiggled Gabryl's thick brows suggestively at DUNO, sending a homoerotic wave of heat through the gun-toting, closeted punk. DUNO had already been tried as an adult and as soon as he fucked up enough he'd be heading back to jail, back into the cycle of sexual abuse he'd blocked out as a kid that had started both his and his brother's dark descent.

The spirit riding Gabryl blew a thick-mouthed kiss at DUNO and stuck his tongue out the corner of his mouth, rolling his eyes up to pantomime being dead.

DUNO exploded in a panicked, confused dance of lunging towards him and falling back all at once, right when the cops got about a yard away. His brother NONO grabbed him and pushed him into the crowd, passing the gun over to Lookout and slickly down the line into the school unnoticed.

"DUNO, come on man!"  NONO yelled  then narrowed his eyes at Gabryl standing nonplussed. "Fucking skinhead little punk bitch-"  he hissed over his shoulder, the only one of the crew in the right grade.

"What?! No-No Double Negative? Damn-I-I feel cheated! I-" Gabryl stopped mid-sentence.

"Woaw !Now I feel like I - I Know nothing-" the Aware in Gabryl called out after him as NONO walked away.

A cop bloomed up in Gabryl's face, absently reminding him of someone he couldn't place. "What?" he asked and shrugged his shoulders defensively.

"School, Son." The cop stated slowly, like he was talking to an idiot. "Go. To. School. And wash your face- you got silver shit glowing on your forehead," the cop called out as Gabryl moved along.

The Aware in Gabryl yawned and passed back out as his angry, rage-filled panic took hold again.  He stomped into the high school.

As soon as he crossed the threshold the two little inner kids that were once him ran the rest of the way up the block and parted ways, running for their collective lives.

**chapter fifty**

Two floors and a wing away, Tigris was getting pissed.

"Yo Mateo!" Tigris hissed into his walkie-talkie, "What the-
this is why she's always-"

At the sound of the voice of Tigris, La Magra took off in his
direction instead of the exit as Mateo jogged behind her.

Tigris slammed the button on the handheld to stop himself
from saying stuff he knew he shouldn't in the presence of
children. He spun around, feeling the eyes of the five year olds
glaring at him due to his bad energy.

"What?!" Tigris snapped.
*That's what we were about to ask you~*" a few yelled
telepathically at him, scowling.

"You want to know what's wrong with me?" he railed. "This!"
he roared, pointing accusingly at the painting of Cupid and
Psyche as kids that he was always assigned to guard in the
gallery. "This-is what's wrong! It-it shouldn't have to be that
way-"

The little spirit of La Magra sprinted into the room and skipped
around before she leaped up onto him like a tree squirrel
and planted a bloodied kiss firmly on his forehead, stunning
him to silence.

She held his face with her sticky hands and peered into his eyes
until he calmed down, then hopped off of him and pirouetted
out of the gallery, Mateo on her heels to push her dance back
towards the exit.

A soft hush fell over Tigris and all the kids in the room, who could see the spirit kid as easily as they could see each other. One of the little kids cooed. The others joined in with her, making Tigris blush.

"Awww~"

"Get back to work!" he growled then slowly followed after La Magra and Mateo, stupefied by how easily the spirit of the little kid had soothed him, like she knew who'd been looking out for her all along  in this place.

When Mateo and la Magra got to the portico, most of the blood that hadn't rinsed away had flaked off of the both of them. The Little Blood God tried to dash through the two guards waiting to ensure her exit, but Rubio tripped her.

 Santiago lifted the ruby-crusted blade and other artifacts she knew better than to play with off her body. She giggled and dove onto a waiting Anukai, who gathered the rest of herself together like a mother hen and then stood up.

Anukai smiled sarcastically at Mateo and Tigris slowly coming towards the cluster of them, knowing neither had seen exactly whom she'd literally grown up into.  Mateo tried to find words to ask how old she was but only a hoarse whistle came out. In shock, Mateo went to step towards her but Santiago stopped him.

"Boy, you know you have asthma outside of here," Santiago muttered, watching the young man marvel at how the light hit her like she was the only one he'd ever need to see for the rest of his time here.

"And her Guardian would rip the foundations of this place out over you thinking what is on your face-" Rubio whispered, laughing.  When Anukai saw they were not going to allow Mateo to step to her all the way for the good of them both, she cockily stepped towards him.

"Depends ...How old are you?" she flirted telepathically.

Santiago popped her in her third eye to interrupt her. Anukai stepped back, cutting her eyes like the child she still officially was in their eyes right as Tigris got close enough to see her.

The little girl who'd just kissed him on the forehead in the gallery stood there rubbing her own next to the young woman she had quietly become. His jaw dropped in disbelief as her eyes went white watching him try not to spin out internally. The wind kicked up out of nowhere, making all parties step away from each other.  "Go to school!" Rubio yelled as the doors slammed shut right  in Anukai's face.

Anukai snorted and began to head  towards school, hearing Santiago's trill dance over her shoulder and  across the lagoon.

"And you~ what took you so long?" he barked accusingly at Tigris and Mateo. "And put OUT of your mind how she was eye to eye with you now!"

Mateo and Tigris sheepishly made their way back to the gallery with the painting of Cupid and Psyche and stood on either side of it.

Groups of schoolchildren swarmed in and out of the gallery for the rest of the day.

By the end of it, Tigris was still speechless due to his outright shock at the damn-near adult reality of the  childlike spirit that had kissed him on the forehead.

"Is that why our chest feels better?" Tigris asked.

Mateo blushed bright red. "I-I had-no clue she-she was… but yeah.! Damn! How old do *you* think she is now? I know she looked-Grown-but she can't be.. .Can she?"

"Young enough to still obey when two old art guards send her to school." Tigris mumbled back.

"But-I -I mean-" Mateo stammered.
"We have less than six months before we're done, then we-" Tigris interrupted.

"Go home-I know, I know we're not staying here-we're almost done, degree'd-  but-what about-" Mateo started.

"She won't stay. Trust me, when she's grown, she's gone-count on it." Tigris said softly.

For the first time in ages Mateo Tigris was finally in agreement inside of himself over something.

The two gallery guards looked at each other and then began to walk towards one another, stepping into one for the first time in forever.

The children drawing on the floor in the gallery looked up as everything in the room shifted, then went  back to their projects.

**chapter fifty one**

"Now where were we?" the woman purred into the ear of one she'd left in the pile.

He readily nuzzled back in where he had been. She bit her jaw again, toes curling from the pain that faded in a surge of ecstasy double-helixing through her lower regions. Blood flooded into her numbed hips with such force that she cried out, body awakened.

The sound of her toy's erratic heartbeat was treble to the bass of the Ka's *So Be It* echoing in her head.

Progressive house shook the Bunker. Her lashes were sticky with desire, for more than those who thought they'd just feed. Her mind ran across expanses of other Awares also shooting in barrels. A desire that could never be quenched by the empty calories of these Latents growled within her.

Each gasp of heat was loaded with this hollow hope of deeper, of more.

"Of ~Chrysalis-" the woman whispered to herself. Her eyes slid all the way closed.

"So Be it." her Ka whispered back.

Everything around the woman exploded into a fireball of hail, charred bones and ash as her Ba instantly was encased in a Kagome latticework of quartz.


**The end.**

## ABOUT THE AUTHOR

Author and multimedia artist Angel Brynner has marched to the beat of her own drum across the arts for over two decades. After formal training with the vanguard of the menswear industry she helmed her own line of men's clothing and produced events  for the collection in the club scenes of New York and Tokyo.

She became quietly known for the futuristic cautionary tales back-dropping her collections, taking over clubs and the guerilla-marketing style she used to slam her vision into the hearts of her fans. While being sponsored by Multinational companies desiring audience with her underground tribe, she returned from Japan to her hometown to press charges against a pedophile before the statute of limitations ran out.

Cast as a vigilante by a corrupt sex crimes unit for trying to protect another child from the same attacker, during the media onslaught against the first brave adults to come forward and press charges against the Catholic priests that had abused them as children she was hit with a vision of all those already lost in a sick war on kids no one talked about.

She committed herself & her art to doing something about it.

The grievechronic universe was forged in the fires of imagining the Armageddon that would erupt through a generation of kids who had finally had enough abuse at the hands of adults and banded together under their grievances.

The epic spiritual, metaphysical, and historical implications of such an event played out on every level- from the hellish norms that caused it to what would be called heaven by such a broken world- made her head spin.

Epicharis, a fever-dream of a book published by Kokopellima Press, is the seventh free-standing installment of the  take-no- prisoners tale.

Alongside  AOLAB[the active-art series  featuring the multimedia work that fed Eutaxis, Ecclesia, Exodus, Erebus, Exist and the kinetic collection of novels that follow them], Angel Brynner's books are the culmination of an artistic journey many years in the making, all leading to a mysterious future project entitled *Transcendence*.

Artyo wakes up in the bowels of the Highest High
spitting bullets out into her lap as the bane of her
violent, broken hearted existence in
Hell on Earth looms over her.

Can Death become a point of Passover
that revokes every aspect nefariously hidden
on the first run through?

…And what good does that kind of truth ever lead to?

Some things don't get healed until the brains all over the
place are sifted through. And no matter what,
where never means as much as what we went through
trying to get there.

Love can be ignored, suppressed, neglected or
omitted…but everything stricken
from the record rises
in direct relation to the escape velocity
of a spirit slamming out of hell.

**Want more of the grievechronic universe?**

Email <u>info@kokopellimapress.com</u>

For access to exclusive, free and

special edition goods tied to

All things grievechronic.

…and check out www.grievechronic.com

KOKOPELLIMA PRESS

www.ingramcontent.com/pod-product-compliance
Lightning Source LLC
Chambersburg PA
CBHW070944190726
48292CB00004B/1338